#7 The King and Us

Look for these and other books
in the Bad News Ballet series:

Bad News Ballet

#7 The King and Us

Jahnna N. Malcolm

AN
APPLE
PAPERBACK

SCHOLASTIC INC.
New York Toronto London Auckland Sydney

For Aunt Gertie
with love

ISBN 0-590-43395-4

12 11 10 9 8 7 6 5 4 3 2 1   0 1 2 3 4 5/9

Printed in the U.S.A.   11

First Scholastic printing, April 1990

Chapter One

"We've just heard the most disgusting news!" Rocky Garcia declared as she stormed into the dressing room of the Deerfield Academy of Dance.

A tall, thin black girl was right on Rocky's heels. "It's truly terrible," Zan Reed breathed in her soft voice.

"Yeah, it makes me gag!" a short, plump redhead called from behind Rocky and Zan. Gwendolyn Hays limped to the nearest bench and fumbled with the ribbons on her toe shoes.

Their Saturday ballet class had just ended and the dressing room was crowded with fifth- and sixth-grade girls changing out of their leotards. A curly-headed blonde sat down on the bench beside Gwen.

1

"I can't stand the suspense," Mary Bubnik drawled in her Oklahoma accent. "Tell us the news."

"First let me get out of these awful shoes," Gwen replied. She shoved her wire-rimmed glasses up on her nose and winced. "It feels like someone put little tiny pins in each of the toes."

"I think someone put pins in all of our shoes," Kathryn McGee announced. She had been the first one of their gang into the dressing room and had already removed her pink satin slippers. McGee hopped over to the bench and thrust her foot into Gwen's line of vision. "And they tore a hole right through my tights." She wiggled her big toe that stuck out of the end of her faded pink tights. "Look, a callus is starting to form."

"I'm not surprised." Gwen squinched up her nose and shoved McGee's toe away from her face. "You've got calluses everywhere else."

"But those are from playing baseball." McGee examined the rough patches of skin on her hands critically. Swinging the bat in Little League had made her hands tough and leathery. She flipped one of her chestnut braids over her shoulder. "I thought ballet was supposed to make you soft and graceful."

"No way." Rocky yanked the rubber band out of her thick black hair, and it exploded into a fuzzy dark cloud around her face. "Ballet only makes you mad."

Mary Bubnik sighed impatiently. "I wish y'all would tell McGee and me what's got you so upset."

Gwen, Rocky, and Zan exchanged meaningful

2

looks. Then they turned back to their friends and said in unison, "The Bunheads!"

Bunhead was the nickname the girls had given the snobby ballerinas in their dance class who wore their hair pulled into tight knots on top of their heads and acted like they were better than anyone else.

"Now I understand." Mary Bubnik nodded her head slowly. "But what have they done this time?"

"Yeah, they seemed to be okay in dance class today." McGee leaned into the tight huddle the five girls had formed in the corner of the dressing room. "I mean, Courtney was her usual snotty self, hogging the center of the dance floor."

"And Page Tuttle was a big show-off, always volunteering to demonstrate the new steps," Mary chimed in.

"And Alice Wescott was just a little tagalong behind Courtney and Page, trying to do her *grand battement* kicks higher than the rest of us." McGee shrugged her shoulders. "But that's nothing new. Those guys are like that in every class."

"We're not talking about what happened *in* class," Rocky cut in. "We're talking about what we heard *afterward.*"

"Right," Gwen said, massaging her foot as she narrowed her eyes at McGee. "You were in such a hurry to be first into the dressing room that you missed the whole thing."

McGee rolled her eyes at the ceiling. "Well, if you don't tell me what happened soon, I'll go directly to

3

the Bunheads and ask *them* what they did that was so awful."

"You can't," Zan replied. "They're in Mr. Anton's office, talking over their parts in *Sleeping Beauty*."

"What?" Mary Bubnik's eyes were two big blue circles in her head. "They've been cast in the company's new ballet?"

"You got it," Rocky said, slipping into her black Levi's. She stuffed her arms into her red satin jacket with her name printed in silver letters across the back. "And they didn't even have to audition."

"That's not fair!" McGee groaned.

"We heard Annie Springer telling them the news just as we were leaving the studio," Zan explained. "Annie will be dancing the role of Aurora, the Sleeping Beauty." She sighed. "I bet she'll be truly wonderful."

The rest of the gang nodded in agreement. Annie Springer was their teacher and one of the leading dancers of the Deerfield Ballet.

"Remember how good she was as the Sugar Plum Fairy in *The Nutcracker*?" Mary Bubnik remarked.

Zan squeezed her eyes shut tightly. "I can still see her now, pirouetting in that beautiful tutu."

The gang had first met in November when the Deerfield Ballet held auditions for *The Nutcracker*. None of the girls had wanted to be in the ballet, but their mothers had made them try out. The experience had been terrible at first, but they soon banded together to battle the Bunheads and had been fast friends ever since.

"Do you remember how unbearable the Bunheads were?" Rocky grumbled.

"Just because Courtney and her friends were chosen to be in the 'Waltz of the Flowers,' " Mary Bubnik said, "they thought they were so cool."

"It didn't help any that we were·cast as the rats," Gwen remarked.

"They never let us live that down," Zan moaned.

"Now that they've been chosen to be in another ballet," Rocky continued, "they're going to be impossible to be around."

"This is too depressing." Gwen leaned over and picked up her blue canvas dance bag. "I need a Twinkie." She dug in the side pocket and promptly produced three packages of snack cakes. "Anybody else want one? I've also got Ding Dongs and Ho Hos."

"Ding Dongs and Ho Hos?" McGee repeated as she pulled her baseball jersey out of her dance bag. "What happened to your diet?"

"I just blew it." Gwen peeled back the plastic wrapper and bit into the spongy cake.

"Wow!" Rocky shook her head in amazement. "When you blow it, you blow it big."

"Right," Gwen mumbled with a full mouth. "Never do anything halfway, that's my motto."

"What parts are the Bunheads playing in *Sleeping*

Beauty?" McGee asked, slipping on her jersey. It had "Fairview Red Sox" written across the chest.

"The royal ring bearers," Zan replied.

Gwen swallowed hard. "Sounds like a circus act."

"Well, it's not," Rocky grumbled. "They're featured parts in the academy's biggest ballet *ever*."

Mary Bubnik narrowed her eyes suspiciously. "Courtney's mother must have gotten her in the ballet."

"That's not true!" Courtney Clay stood framed in the doorway with her arms crossed. Her lips were pursed in a pout that made her look like she'd just eaten a lemon. "You're just saying that because you're jealous."

"Jealous! Of you?" Rocky snorted. "That's a laugh."

Gwen took a final bite of her Twinkie and then calmly licked her fingers as she spoke. "We do find it interesting that your mother just *happens* to be on the board of directors, and you and your two friends just *happened* to be chosen to be in the ballet, and no one else was even given a chance to try out."

Courtney watched as Gwen opened another snack cake. "Mr. Anton needed dancers who could fit in the costumes," she replied snidely. Then Courtney stalked across the room in the telltale turned-out walk of a ballet dancer. The other girls in the class parted to make way for her as she took her place at the dressing table.

6

McGee caught the hurt look on Gwen's face and called out, "So, Courtney, you got the part because you could fit in the dress?"

Courtney, who had leaned forward to peer at her reflection in the mirror, spun around angrily. "Mr. Anton also needed *good* dancers — which you most certainly are *not*."

"Good dancers?" Rocky retorted. "How hard can it be to be a royal ring bearer?"

"Go ahead and laugh," Page Tuttle called from the doorway. The slender blonde dancer was Courtney's best friend. "*We*'ll be up on stage getting all that applause, while *you*'ll be in the audience turning green with envy."

"Yeah," Alice Wescott added, sticking her head through the curtain behind Page. The mousy little fourth-grader stuck out her tongue and jeered in her whiny voice, "Eat your heart out."

"By the way, Courtney, Mr. Anton wants to see us again," Page announced in an extra loud voice. "We need to schedule rehearsals and costume fittings, and talk about helping out at the opening night gala."

"I'll be right there," Courtney trilled as she swept past the gang and disappeared through the curtain with her friends.

The gang waited until the Bunheads were gone, then slumped back against the lockers. A gray cloud of gloom seemed to hover over the tiny cubicle. Even the other girls in the class seemed downcast from the news of the Bunheads' triumph. The gang sat despondently while the rest of their class finished dressing in silence and left the room.

"It's already started," Zan said once the five of them were alone. "For the next three months, and maybe for the whole rest of the year, all we'll ever hear is how terrific it was to get picked for parts in *Sleeping Beauty.*"

"They get to help out at the gala, and everything," Mary Bubnik murmured sadly. "I bet we won't even be invited."

"Who cares?" Rocky muttered darkly. "It's still just a stupid ballet. I thought we hated ballet." She looked at the others for agreement. "Right?"

No one said a word. McGee just sat on the changing bench in her baseball jersey and high-tops, staring down at the floor.

Gwen was about to open another package of snack cakes, when she stopped and shoved them back into her bag. "This is awful," she declared glumly. "I'm too depressed to even *eat.*"

The curtain to the dressing room rustled and a slight, elderly woman came into the room. The gang didn't even look up but continued sitting silently by their lockers.

"Vat is go-ink on here?" the woman asked in a lilting Russian accent. She wore a·lavender caftan and matching brocade turban. The ends of the bright red chiffon scarf around her neck streamed behind her as she walked. "You girls look like someone has died."

"We wish," Rocky mumbled.

"I guess you haven't heard the bad news, Miss Delacorte," Zan said, smiling mournfully at the academy's receptionist. "About the Bunheads, that is."

A small smile crept across Miss Delacorte's face at the use of their nickname. Earlier in the year, she had had her own problems with those girls when Courtney and her minions had tried to get her fired. The gang had come to the old woman's defense, and they had become good friends.

Then her smile quickly faded. "Yes, I heard. It seems so very unfair." Miss Delacorte fluttered one thin, bony hand. "But you girls should not feel bad. All the royal ring bearers have to do in *Sleep-ink Beauty* is appear at the end for a few minutes, stand on ze stage, and hold a little satin pillow. No danc-ink is required."

"But they get to be in the ballet," Mary Bubnik protested.

"And wear beautiful costumes," Zan moaned.

"And get their picture in the newspaper," Rocky said.

"And go to the gala," McGee added wistfully.

"And eat all of those great hors d'oeuvres," Gwen finished.

"Well, if all you want is to appear in a costume on the stage, and eat cheese and crackers at the opening night party," Miss Delacorte replied, "perhaps you will be interested in this." She held up a white sheet of paper with an announcement typed in the

9

center. "I *vas* just about to post this on the bulletin board."

The girls gathered around their friend as Zan read the announcement out loud. "The Carousel Dinner Theatre will be holding open auditions for their upcoming production of the musical *The King and I*."

McGee took over reading the note on the board. "Needed: boys and girls between the ages of six and twelve, to play the roles of the King's children. Some dancing and singing required. The production opens in two weeks and will star Nicholas Blade — "

"Nicholas Blade!" Zan gasped in amazement. "He's my favorite TV star. I watch him every afternoon after school."

"That's just because he plays a private eye," Gwen said. "You're a sucker for detectives."

That was true. Zan eagerly read every detective and mystery book she could lay her hands on. Her favorites were the *Tiffany Truenote, Teen Detective* stories. She'd read them so many times she practically had them memorized.

"The main reason *I* love him," Mary Bubnik cut in, "is because he's such a *hunk*." She sighed dreamily. "Did you ever see such blue, blue eyes?"

"If you like this Nicholas fellow so much, why don't you girls try out for the show?" Miss Delacorte crossed to the wall by the dressing table and tacked the announcement on the cork bulletin board. "All you have to do is dance a lee-tle dance and sing a lee-tle song." As she sailed through the curtained door, the receptionist called over her shoulder, "Vat could be easier?"

As the gang hurriedly pulled on the rest of their clothes, Zan turned to the others and asked, "Do you think it's really possible for us to get cast in that play?"

"Sure," McGee said confidently as she pulled her baseball breeches over her shoes.

"I could work on our acting techniques," Rocky declared. Rocky took acting lessons at the recreation center on Curtiss-Dobbs Air Force Base where she lived. She had also been in several plays. The group considered her their drama expert.

"And I could play the piano for our song," said Gwen, who'd taken lessons since she was four.

"It would be truly wonderful!" Zan gushed.

"And the perfect way to show the slime Courtney Clay that we're as good as she is." Gwen was still smarting from the comment Courtney had made about her weight.

"We're *better*," Rocky crowed. "Because we're going to be on the stage with the world-famous actor Nicholas Blade!"

"Star of *Nicholas Blade, Private Eye*," Zan cried, clasping her hands together.

Everyone cheered except Mary Bubnik. "I don't want to be a wet blanket, or anything," she said finally, "but couldn't the Bunheads try out for this?"

11

McGee's face fell. "She's right. Courtney and Page could read this notice, go audition, and beat us out of these parts, too."

"Oh, no!" Zan moaned in a low voice. "That would be too, too terrible to imagine."

There was an uneasy silence as they contemplated the humiliation they would suffer if that occured.

Finally Gwen said flatly, "We just won't tell them about it. And then we'll work really hard on our audition."

"And just to be on the safe side" — Rocky looked over both shoulders and then ripped the announcement off the bulletin board — "I'll just *borrow* this for a while," she said with a grin, tucking it inside her red satin jacket. "And they'll never know the auditions existed."

"Way to go!" McGee gave Rocky a high five. "Now we'll see who's jealous of who."

"I say we go to Hi Lo's and celebrate," Gwen declared. The little restaurant across the street from the studio was owned by their special friend, Mr. Lo. Gwen's appetite had returned, and she could already picture herself downing a huge chocolate sundae.

"I can't hang out for long," McGee said as they moved to the black curtain hanging across the dressing room door. "I've got a Little League game later this afternoon."

"That's OK," Zan said, looping her leather bag over her shoulder. "We'll just stay long enough to plan our strategy for getting cast in *The King and I.*"

"Good idea," Mary said. "Because I have one more piece of bad news to tell y'all."

The girls stopped in their tracks and turned slowly to face her.

"What?" McGee asked.

"Well, not only am I a pretty lousy dancer, but . . ." Mary Bubnik hesitated.

"But what?" Rocky asked.

"I can't sing."

Chapter Two

Minutes later, the gang stood in front of a small restaurant that sat wedged between two tall buildings. A friendly red-and-white sign that hung above the entrance proclaimed, "Hi Lo's Pizza and Chinese Food to Go."

As Gwen shoved open the glass door, a tiny brass bell signaled their arrival. The girls stepped inside and looked around. The little café was deserted. There was a vacant booth against the back wall and six empty stools lined the luncheon counter.

Rocky cupped her hands around her mouth and bellowed, "Hey, we'd like some service here! What kind of a joint is this?"

A small Chinese man with round glasses and a tall, white chef's hat stuck his head through the serving window from the kitchen. His lined face creased into a broad grin as he recognized them. "Greetings and salutations, my friends!"

"Hi, Hi!" McGee called as she hopped onto one of the red leather stools. "How's it going?" The other four imitated McGee and clustered around the curved counter.

"Up till now, it's been pretty boring," the old man replied. "But you are just the people I wanted to see."

"Yeah?" Rocky looked up in interest. "What for?"

Hi Lo held up one finger in the air and assumed a mysterious air. "One moment, please." He ducked his head back inside and seconds later burst through the swinging door from the kitchen. His apron was covered in splotches of purple and red and a broad swath of flour lay across one cheek. "I have spent the entire morning working on my latest Hi Lo Special," he explained, setting a huge platter on the counter in front of them. "And now I need some experts to give it a taste-test."

"Experts?" Rocky stared at the platter dubiously. A large crusty blob of dough sat in the middle of it. "Guinea pigs, is more like it."

"Gee, Hi, it looks really, um ..." Mary Bubnik paused as she tried to think of something nice to say about the shapeless mass before her. "Different."

"You are quite right, Mary Bubnik." Hi beamed at the five girls proudly. "I have never tried anything like this before. I combined several of my favorite recipes that have been handed down from generation to generation."

"From China?" Zan asked, imagining people hundreds of years before making this same recipe.

Hi looked at her in surprise. "Oh, my, no," he said with a chuckle, "these are pure Betty Crocker. I added my own special touch, and now I call it the May Day Surprise."

"Did you put any secret ingredients in it?" Gwen asked cautiously. Hi had a habit of adding little extras to his specials that made them uniquely his. Sometimes they were delicious, like pieces of cantaloupe in a vanilla shake; and sometimes they were just weird, like apples in tomato sauce, or peanut butter and onion sandwiches.

"I most certainly did." Hi gestured proudly to the lump that sat on the tray. "Then I covered it in a light pastry crust and baked it in the oven." He pulled out a long knife from beneath the counter and aimed it at the center of the mound. "Now we shall see how it turned out."

Ka-*boom*! The moment the knife penetrated the crust, a spray of lemon pudding shot up and covered the lenses of Hi's glasses. A cloud of flour billowed around the room, and the girls stared in amazement as the ball of dough deflated with a pathetic wheeze. Melted ice cream, mixed with nuts and raisins, and thick chocolate syrup oozed out onto the counter.

"Barf-o-rama!" Gwen gasped, nearly falling backwards off the stool.

"Wow!" McGee exclaimed. "That was amazing."

Mary Bubnik nodded. "Like a small, gooey volcano."

Hi wiped the lemon pudding off his glasses with a dish towel. "That's the third time that has happened," he remarked, a perplexed look on his face. "I'm not sure what's going wrong."

"If it explodes like that on the counter," Rocky murmured, "just imagine what it does in your stomach."

Hi held up several long-handled spoons. "Would you like to taste it?"

"No!" all five girls cried at once. Their reply was so forceful that Hi stepped back from the counter.

"I can't," Gwen said hastily. "I'm dieting."

"So am I!" Mary Bubnik chimed in.

"We all are!" McGee added, gesturing with her arm to include Rocky and Zan.

Hi raised an eyebrow at Zan, who was as thin as a rail.

Mary Bubnik hurriedly tried to change the subject. "You see, we have a big audition coming up on Monday," she said breathlessly, "and we need to be in perfect health."

"Yeah," Rocky muttered under her breath, "we need to be alive." McGee planted a stiff elbow squarely in Rocky's ribs. "Ow!" she yelped. "That hurts!"

"That's not polite," McGee whispered.

"Well, if you're so set on being polite," Rocky retorted, clutching her side, "why don't *you* taste it?"

"No way!" McGee blurted out. Then she blushed and looked back at Hi, who'd overheard their entire conversation. "I mean, well . . ."

"You don't have to worry about hurting my feelings," the old man reassured them with a smile. "Frankly, it doesn't look very appetizing to me, either."

"I hate to say it, Hi," Gwen said, poking at the melted goo with a straw from the metal dispenser, "but your May Day Surprise looks pretty gross."

"Well, I think May Day Surprise is the perfect name for it," Zan declared. When the girls looked at her blankly, she explained, "Pilots always radio May Day when a disaster strikes and they need to bail out."

Suddenly Hi started giggling. The laughter started at his head, then his shoulders began bouncing up and down. Soon his whole body was bent over bobbing with laughter. "It's a good thing no customers were here to see the explosion," he gasped through his giggles. "They'd probably never come back."

"You'd have to change your restaurant's name to Hi Lo's Pizza and Chinese Food to *Blow*," Gwen cracked.

That made them all burst out laughing. Hi pounded Gwen on the back. "That's a good one!"

"That would make a great surprise to send to your enemies," Mary Bubnik cried, wiping tears of laughter out of her eyes.

"A real secret weapon," Hi agreed.

18

"Hey, maybe you can make one a little stronger, and we could send it to the Bunheads," Rocky suggested with a wicked grin. "I'd love to see the look on their faces when the lemon pudding blows their toe shoes off."

That prompted another gale of laughter.

"Then they couldn't be in *Sleeping Beauty*," Gwen said.

"And we wouldn't have to audition for *The King and I*," Mary Bubnik added.

Hi stopped chuckling. "What's this about *The King and I*?"

Zan explained about the auditions at the Carousel Dinner Theatre and added with a sigh, "It stars Nicholas Blade — my hero."

"Nicholas Blade, Private Eye?" Hi looked very impressed. "I watch his re-runs every afternoon on TV." He checked his watch and announced, "In fact, the Saturday afternoon show should be on now."

"Oooh, Hi!" Mary Bubnik pointed to the television set perched on a shelf above the back booth. "Turn it on, so we can look at him."

Hi reached under the counter and pulled out the remote control. He hit a button and the TV flickered on. The theme music for *Nicholas Blade, Private Eye* filled the restaurant as the credits scrolled across the screen. "Too bad. It's ending," Hi said.

He started to turn it off, but Zan held up her hand. "Please, don't turn it off! I like this part. They show highlights of his past adventures."

19

As the credits rolled, a tan, muscular guy in a yachting cap waved at the camera from a speed boat. In the next picture, the detective was seen dangling from a rope off a cliff. In yet another, he was at the wheel of his Jaguar sports car, speeding around a mountain curve.

"This next is my favorite," Zan said as the camera zoomed in for a close-up of Nicholas Blade winking and giving a thumbs-up into the lens.

"He is *soooooo* handsome!" Mary Bubnik squealed.

Zan rested her chin on her hands and said dreamily, "I wonder if he's married."

"I wonder if he can sing," Hi said, taking the tray to the sink behind the counter and pouring the melted remains of the May Day Surprise down the drain. "*The King and I* is a very big musical."

"Of course he can sing," Zan said, sitting up straight.

Mary Bubnik nodded. "Nicholas Blade can do anything."

"We have to get into that show," Gwen declared, slapping her palm emphatically against the counter.

"Right. Now, the audition is on Monday," McGee said. "And we have to do a little dance and sing a song. What should we sing?"

Zan dug in her tapestry bag for her lavender pad. She pulled the cap off her pen with her teeth and sat poised, ready to take notes.

"I like rap," Rocky said, beating out a rhythm on

the countertop. "We can work out some great moves that'll knock their socks off."

"But that won't show the director that we can sing," Zan pointed out. "We need something with a real recognizable tune."

"You mean like 'I'm a Little Teapot'?" Mary Bubnik asked.

"Something like that," Gwen said. "But not that."

McGee raised her hand. "How about something traditional, like 'My Country 'Tis of Thee'?"

"That's a good one," Zan said, writing the title down. "It also shows that we're patriotic."

" 'I'm a Little Teapot' is *very* traditional," Mary Bubnik persisted. "I mean, *my* parents sang it, and *their* parents sang it, and *their* parents before them."

"And I bet they all felt stupid," Gwen said. "Especially if they did the dumb movements that go with it."

Mary twisted one of her curls around her finger. "I think those movements are kind of fun," she murmured.

"We'd look like a bunch of geeks," Rocky said with a brisk shake of her head. "Remember, we need to get cast in this play to show the Bunheads we're better than them. 'I'm a Little Teapot' just won't cut it."

"More important, we need to show the director how good we are," Zan reminded them. "Choice of material is very important in this sort of thing."

"Well, I hope the director doesn't mind people who

are tone-deaf," Mary Bubnik said, slumping forward onto the counter. " 'Cause that's me."

"I'm sure that's not true," Zan reassured her. "Everyone can sing *something*."

Mary Bubnik shook her head firmly. "Not me. I can't sing a thing. Except..."

She paused and the others finished her sentence with a loud groan: " ... 'I'm a Little Teapot.' "

"Right." Mary Bubnik put her hand over her mouth and giggled. "Back in Oklahoma, the choir director at my church asked me if I would mind just mouthing the words to the hymns, since my singing was throwing everyone off."

"Well, that was just one person. What did he know?" Rocky said, trying her best to sound encouraging.

"Then the head of the Glee Club at my school suggested I try playing the clarinet in the band instead of singing," Mary continued. "But even that didn't work out. My fingers were too uncoordinated, and my mom told me she was going to have a nervous breakdown if I played one more note at home."

"What did you do?" Zan asked.

"I quit music altogether and took up art. But that was even worse." Mary Bubnik was about to tell them her disastrous experience in art class when they heard a tinkling sound as the door from the street opened.

"Saved by the bell," Rocky whispered to Gwen. She really liked Mary Bubnik, but once Mary got started telling one of her stories, she never seemed to stop.

Two boys stepped inside the restaurant. Their red-and-white warm-up jackets had "Fairview Red Sox" stenciled in red letters across the chest, just like McGee's jersey. Each boy had a baseball glove tucked under his arm and a red baseball cap on his head.

"Hey, it's McGee," one of them said. He was a lanky boy with curly blond hair and a dimple in his cheek. McGee spun around on her stool as he trotted over to her side and gave her a low five.

"Hey, Lorenzen," McGee answered back. "What are you doing here? You should be warming up your arm for the game."

The boy looped his arm over her shoulder. "Who needs to warm up? We're playing the Kettering Wildcats. Those turkeys couldn't bat their way out of a paper bag."

McGee flipped up the brim of her baseball cap and grinned. "Yeah, I heard they really got pasted last week."

"Twenty-five to nothing," he said. "A complete shutout."

While the boy ordered two Cokes to go, his friend, who had short dark hair and a chipped tooth, leaned easily against the counter talking to McGee. "Spi-

23

noza said you've been working out with weights. How come? You're already the best catcher in the league."

"Coach thought some extra strength would speed up my throw to second," McGee explained. She flexed her bicep and held it out for him to feel it. "I think the weights helped."

The dark-haired boy's eyes widened as he felt her muscle. "Whoa! That's intense."

After Lorenzen paid Hi for their Cokes, he smiled vaguely at the gang and then punched McGee on the shoulder. "See you in the dugout, partner."

"Right."

The boys were barely out of the building before Gwen blurted out, "That has got to be the cutest boy I've ever seen. What's his name?"

"Chris Lorenzen," McGee said quietly. "He's our pitcher."

Rocky whistled low. "That is one cool dude."

"You're telling me," Mary Bubnik giggled. She leaned over and whispered loudly into McGee's ear, "And he really seems to like you."

McGee shrugged. "As a friend. But that's it."

"How can you say that?" Mary Bubnik protested. "We saw him put his arm around you."

"He wouldn't do that if he didn't really like you," Zan pointed out.

"He also punched me on the arm and talked about baseball." McGee slumped down on the counter.

"That's the story of my life. As far as Chris is concerned, I'm just one of the guys."

"At least he talks to you," Gwen said. "The only time a guy talks to me is when he's hungry. They all know I have an extra supply of snacks in my locker." Gwen added hastily, "For emergencies."

"I know tons of boys," McGee continued, "and they all think of me as their buddy. They talk to me about their girlfriends and then have me pass notes to them in class. The only time I get asked out is when they want to practice their swing, or try out a new pitch." She sighed heavily. "I don't know what to do."

"Do nothing," Hi called from inside the kitchen.

"What?" McGee protested. "Why?"

Hi popped his head out the serving window. "Excuse me for butting in, but I like you just the way you are — and so do the boys. If they like you as a friend now — later they will like you as a girlfriend, and someday one will love you as a wife."

McGee rolled her eyes. "That sounds like something my mother would say."

"Your mother must be a very wise woman," Hi remarked, then popped his head back inside.

"Geez Louise," McGee muttered under her breath.

Then the swinging door flew open and Hi reappeared with another tray. "Here you are, ladies, five chocolate sundaes on the house."

Rocky looked at them suspiciously and Hi reassured her, "With no special name, and no secret ingredients."

"That's more like it," Gwen said, eagerly picking up her spoon.

McGee hopped off her stool. "Sorry, guys, I can't stay. I have a game to get to."

"That's okay," Gwen said as she slid McGee's bowl toward her and dug her spoon into the ice cream. "I'll eat yours for you."

McGee picked up her glove and headed for the door. "I'll catch you guys at the audition Monday."

"Wait a minute!" Rocky called after her. "We haven't decided what we're going to do."

McGee paused with one hand on the glass door handle. "What are our options?"

Zan looked down at the pad. "Well, right now we only have two possibilities. 'I'm a Little Teapot' and 'My Country 'Tis of Thee.' "

McGee grinned. "Well, the choice is obvious. why don't we all practice at home?" Before anyone could say another word, she was out the door. "See you at the audition!"

Chapter Three

"Wow, this is a zoo!" Gwen said as the girls filed into the backstage lounge of the Carousel Dinner Theatre on Monday.

Children of all ages sprawled on the tiled floor, chattering noisily. Meanwhile their mothers had taken up all of the available seats in the cramped room. Four of them sat side by side on an old gray Naugahyde couch in the corner, while three others shared an armchair by the door, one on the cushion with the other two perched on the arms. Another woman wearing a lot of makeup had settled herself among the old magazines littering a rickety coffee table. Everyone was busily filling out audition forms.

"All of Deerfield must have turned out for this thing," Rocky groaned.

"You don't see the Bunheads, do you?" McGee stood on tiptoe and peered over to where several people had gathered along a counter that held a coffee pot and several Styrofoam cups.

Zan, who was the tallest of the gang, shook her head. She could hardly talk. It hadn't occurred to her until this moment that *other* people might attend the auditions, or even worse, they might be *watching* them audition. Her stage fright reappeared with a vengeance. "Are we sure we want to do this?" Zan whispered hoarsely. "I mean, it looks like they've already got all the kids they'll need."

"Of course we want to do this," Mary Bubnik replied, giving Zan a little shove to prod her into the room. "We want to meet Nicholas Blade, don't we?"

At the mention of the TV star, Zan felt goose bumps prickle up and down her arm. She took a deep breath and reminded herself that, after all, Nicholas Blade *was* her hero. She couldn't let a little case of nerves get in the way of meeting him.

"May I have your attention, please?" A chunky girl with cropped blonde hair stood in the doorway behind the gang. She wore a plaid shirt with tan trousers. A dozen keys clinked from a chain hanging from her belt. "I'm Melissa Davidson, the stage

28

manager, and I'll be running the auditions this afternoon. You can call me Mel." She held up a clipboard for everyone to see. "This is the sign-in sheet. I'll leave it here in the green room by the coffee machine."

"This room's not green," Mary Bubnik observed loudly.

Mel heard her and chuckled. "I know it's not. But it's a theatre tradition to call the lounge the 'green room.' Don't ask me why." She shrugged. "Maybe because this is where actors used to get paid after their performances."

"Then they should paint it green so people don't get confused," Mary Bubnik whispered to Rocky, who motioned her to be silent.

"Please print your name clearly on this list," Mel continued. "And then we can begin auditions."

Several of the mothers clutched their children by the hand and rushed forward.

"Jason needs to go first," one of them cried, lifting a startled-looking boy up over the head of the girl in front of him and dropping him at the stage manager's feet.

"Oh, no, you don't!" a large woman in a flowered print dress shouted, shoving her daughter ahead of Jason.

The woman with all the makeup checked her watch and declared, "I absolutely have to leave in half an hour. My daughter must go *now*."

"You should have thought of that before you arrived," another woman shot back. "Timothy and I were here first, and we'll be going first."

The women began to argue shrilly as the stage manager tried to restore order.

"Those are what's known as 'stage mothers,'" Rocky whispered out of the corner of her mouth. "They couldn't be in a play when they were little, so they force their kids to be in them now."

"They're not going to be in the show, are they?" Mary Bubnik asked, imagining how unpleasant that would be.

Rocky waved one hand. "Naw. They'll just hang around before and after rehearsals, getting in everybody's way, until opening night, when the stage manager will make them go sit in the audience where they belong."

A shrill blast from a police whistle brought all the clamor to a standstill. Mel took the whistle from her mouth and smiled pleasantly. "Thank you. As I said, we'll see each child in the order they sign in. No exceptions."

She set the clipboard on the counter and quickly left the room. There was a mad dash as each of the mothers tried to be first to get on the list. McGee and the others worked their way through the crowd and finally were able to write down their names. Then the stage manager brought in some folding chairs, and the gang scrambled to sit in them.

"You girls get audition forms?" Mel asked.

They shook their heads. "We just got here," Gwen explained.

The stage manager handed each of them a form. "Write your name and a phone number where you can be reached at the top. Then list your experience and any conflicts you might have."

A mother sitting on the couch beside a tiny girl with glasses raised her hand. "What kind of experience do you mean?"

Mel ran her hand through her hair. "Any plays or performances the kids might have been in. What kind of dance or voice lessons they've taken — that sort of thing."

"We can put down *The Nutcracker*," Mary Bubnik whispered. "That should impress them."

"Also that we study at the Deerfield Academy of Dance," Zan added. "The best ballet school in Ohio."

As she headed for the door that led to the stage, Mel called over her shoulder, "The director will talk with all of you in just a minute, then we'll begin."

Several teenaged girls sat cross-legged on the floor, using each other's backs as tables to fill out their forms.

"Oh, darn," a pretty blonde with waist-length hair exclaimed, "there's not enough room to list all of the plays I've done. I mean, I put down *Alice in Wonderland* and that took up almost the entire line."

The girl whose back she was using said, "Flip the

paper over. I was able to list all the plays we did at the Deerfield Children's Theatre, plus my work with the puppet group, Hand Jive."

This time it was Mary who murmured, "Gee, maybe Zan's right. Maybe they do have enough experienced people already."

"They're just trying to psych us out," Rocky replied. "Besides, the notice said the director needed kids. Those girls look at least eighteen. I bet they're too old."

Gwen was the first to finish filling out her form. Under "Experience," she had listed *The Nutcracker*, and all her years of piano lessons. For a moment she'd considered mentioning the part she'd played in her science class play at school. But she was afraid the director would ask what it was and then she'd have to tell him she'd been a toad eating flies to demonstrate the food chain. That would be too embarrassing.

Gwen stood up and handed her audition sheet to Mel. Then she spotted several people coming through the stage door and bolted back to her seat with her friends. "Don't look now," she hissed, "but directly behind you is the cutest guy in the whole wide world!"

"Where?" Mary Bubnik started to turn around when Gwen punched her on the shoulder.

"I said, *don't look*," Gwen hissed. "He's standing in the doorway with two other boys."

"Don't worry," Mary said, "I'll be subtle." She grabbed her small pink purse and made a big show of dropping it on the floor. Then she bent down to pick it up, twisting backwards to get a good look at the door. In the process she leaned over too far and her folding chair tipped over, hitting the floor with a loud boom. As she fell, Mary reached out and grabbed Zan by the arm, pulling her down with her.

"Yeow!" Zan shrieked, more in surprise than hurt.

Gwen rolled her eyes at the ceiling. "Very subtle."

McGee rushed over to see if Zan and Mary Bubnik were all right. They were sitting on the floor, giggling like maniacs.

"I can't believe they're doing that," Rocky whispered to Gwen. "They're going to make us all look like a bunch of geeks." Rocky flipped up the collar of her jacket and she and Gwen both slumped down in their folding chairs trying to hide their faces.

As McGee pulled a hysterical Mary to her feet, she looked directly into the cute boy's dark brown eyes. Without thinking, she smiled at him. To her delight he smiled back, and McGee thought she would melt right into the ground.

She completely forgot about Zan, who was sitting on the floor with her hand outstretched, and hurried back to her seat next to Rocky. McGee quickly removed her baseball cap and tried to smooth out the tufts of hair that had come out of her braids. She made a secret vow to herself that, if he talked to her, she wouldn't even mention sports.

"Oh, no!" Rocky whispered. "He's coming this way."

"Don't move!" Gwen gasped.

The boy stepped in front of the girls, put his name on the sign-in sheet, and then stopped in front of McGee. "Aren't you on Fairview's baseball team?" he asked.

Up until that instant McGee had been very proud of her team, and especially of the fact that she was their star catcher. Now she wished she'd never heard of them. McGee bit her lip uncertainly. If she said yes, this cute boy would think she was just another jock, and that would be that.

She hesitated for a second. Finally McGee shook her head. "No. I'm not."

"Oh, gee, I'm sorry." His warm brown eyes were filled with disappointment. "You look just like this girl that plays for them." Then he smiled and added, "She's really terrific."

"Oh, thank — " McGee swallowed hard. How could she thank him? She had to keep pretending it wasn't her. Instead she said, "Do you like sports?"

"Yeah, but I never get to do them much anymore." He gestured toward the stage and added, "Since I've started working here."

Mel reappeared at the stage door. "Say, Brett, the director wants to talk to you for a minute."

The boy named Brett waved in acknowledgment, then turned back to McGee. "Got to go. See you later."

McGee nodded silently. She didn't trust her voice to speak.

"He must be in the play," Gwen said.

"He is," one of the girls sitting across from them declared. "He plays the King's oldest son."

"I wonder how he got that part?" Mary Bubnik wondered out loud. "The auditions haven't even started."

"That's Brett Allen," the blonde said. "He's done tons of shows here. He started in *The Music Man*, and then last year he was one of the leads in *A Thousand Clowns*."

Her friend sighed. "I saw it twice. Brett was great."

Zan, who had managed to pick herself up and sit back in her chair, said, "I think he's cute, but I'm saving myself for Nicholas Blade."

"Me, too," Mary Bubnik agreed. "Now *that's* good-looking."

"All right, listen up, everyone," Mel shouted. "The director wants everyone to come into the theatre. Follow me." There was a nervous scuffling of chairs and papers as everyone jumped up and left the room behind her.

McGee and the gang followed the crowd out into the auditorium. A tall, thin man in jeans and a purple polo shirt was leaning against the stage. A white sweater was looped around his neck, and a pair of sunglasses rested on top of his salt-and-pepper hair. Another pair of reading glasses rested on the top of his nose. He carried stacks of pictures and a worn yellow copy of the script for *The King and I*.

"Good afternoon, everyone," he announced in a deep voice that echoed around the theatre. "I'm Hayden Wilson, the director of this little masterpiece."

A couple of his assistants, who were lounging in the front row seats, chuckled loudly.

"Now, we want to move these auditions along as smoothly as possible," the director continued. "You'll each get your turn, but when Mel, my better half here, says you are through — please, leave the stage." He gestured toward a chubby fellow sitting at an upright piano in the aisle. "Johnny Ogden, our faithful accompanist, will play your sheet music, if you have any. I only want to hear a few bars of a song."

Johnny Ogden, whose red hair looked like someone had stuck a Brillo pad on top of his head, waved pleasantly.

"Basically, what we're looking for today are fifteen Asian children to play our King's kids," Hayden Wilson declared.

There was a loud murmur as the parents and children looked nervously over their shoulders and at the hopefuls milling around them.

"Looks like she's a shoo-in," Rocky whispered, pointing to a tiny Japanese girl who clung to her mother by one of the exits.

The director chuckled loudly. "Obviously, many of you will have to wear makeup to look Asian. But Monty and Cheryl" — he pointed to a boy and girl wearing white smocks — "are our wizards of disguise, and will take care of all that."

The teenaged girls who'd been sitting on the floor talking about their theatre experiences, burst into applause. One of them even shouted, "Way to go, Monty and Cheryl!"

"What is this?" Gwen murmured, "a private club? It looks like everyone already knows each other."

"I know." Mary Bubnik nodded, a worried frown creasing her forehead. "We're never going to get in this play."

"Everyone has an equal chance to be cast," Mr. Wilson announced. "Now I'm looking for energy, energy, *energy*." He pounded his fist in his palm dramatically as he repeated the word. "That's why I've had everyone come into the theatre to watch. We'll be your audience, so I want each of you to give it your best shot."

McGee's eyes turned to huge saucers in her face. "Brett, too?" she whispered to Rocky.

Rocky shrugged. "It looks like it."

McGee shook her head so hard her braids swung across her face. "I can't do it."

37

"Me, neither," Zan gasped, her knees suddenly feeling a little wobbly.

Hayden Wilson gestured to the stage manager, who handed him the piece of paper Gwen had handed her. He glanced at it briefly, then declared, "All right, it looks like Gwendolyn Hays will be first."

"First!" Gwen squeaked. "I — I can't."

The director peered over the top of his half glasses. "What do you mean, you can't?" His voice was ominously low and calm. "If you can't, then what in heaven's name are you doing here?"

Everyone turned to stare at Gwen. She felt her cheeks grow hot with embarrassment and knew she must look like a bright red cherry with freckles. "I mean, I can't do it *alone*." She turned, looking meaningfully at her friends. "Our song is a *group* song."

The director fluttered his hand impatiently. "Whatever. Let's just keep this thing moving."

Zan and McGee had decided to beat a hasty retreat and were headed for the door. But Rocky grabbed each of them firmly by the hand and dragged them up the steps onto the stage. The lights had been turned on and they stood blinking out into the darkness of the auditorium.

"All right, group," the director said sarcastically, "what are you going to do for us today?"

None of them could speak. They hadn't had a chance to discuss their song. Finally Mary Bubnik stepped forward and announced brightly, "We'll be

38

doing 'I'm a Little Teapot.' " She paused, then added, "With all of the movements."

A loud groan sounded from the gang.

"Mark my words, Mary Bubnik," Rocky muttered under her breath. "If we live through this, I'm going to kill you!"

Chapter Four

"Hays Mortuary — you stab 'em, we slab 'em!" Gwen cradled the phone receiver against her ear as she dug into the cookie jar on the kitchen counter. It was Wednesday after school, and the phone had been ringing when she walked into the house. She stuffed a huge oatmeal cookie into her mouth and waited for the caller to respond.

There was a long silence on the other end.

"Hello?" Gwen mumbled with a full mouth. "Anybody there?"

Finally a female voice said brusquely, "I'm trying to reach Gwendolyn Hays. Have I dialed the right number?"

The voice sounded like old lady Phelps, the grumpy secretary at Gwen's school, whom nobody liked. Gwen reached for another cookie and took a loud crunchy bite. "Who wants to know?"

"The Carousel Dinner Theatre."

Gwen's eyes widened, and she nearly choked on her cookie crumbs. After the gang's audition on Monday she'd been convinced they'd never hear from the theatre again. She still got embarrassed thinking about standing on the stage in front of the director, his assistants, and that cute boy, Brett, pretending to be a teapot. It wouldn't have been so bad if Mary hadn't been so off-key. And now some official from the theatre wanted to speak to her, and she'd just acted like a total jerk.

"Uh, just a minute," Gwen said, pretending to be her own sister. "I'll see if Gwen's home yet from her, uh, piano lesson." She put her hand over the phone and shouted loudly, "Gwen, it's for you."

She held the receiver at arm's length and called in a thin, high-pitched cry, as if the voice were coming from the other side of the house, "I'm co-o-o-m-m-ming!"

Then Gwen pointed the receiver down at her feet and ran in place softly, gradually making her footsteps louder to make it sound like she was running to the phone. While she ran Gwen struggled to swallow the rest of her cookie and cleared her throat.

Finally she put the phone up to her mouth, and lowering her voice to what she hoped was a mature tone, said, "This is Gwendolyn Hays."

41

"Gwen? This is Melissa Davidson, the stage manager from the Carousel Dinner Theatre."

"Oh, *hello!*" Gwen affected a surprised tone. Then she added, "I have to apologize for my little sister, who answered the phone. She's not always dealing with a full deck."

Mel chuckled. "That's all right. I just wanted to let you know that you've been cast in *The King and I*."

"I have?" Gwen squealed, forgetting all about disguising her voice. "That's great!"

"The first rehearsal for you will be this Thursday evening at seven P.M."

"Will Nicholas Blade be there?"

"I'm sure he will," Mel replied. "He's already been rehearsing for two weeks."

"Great!" Gwen closed her eyes and imagined the handsome star sitting in one of those canvas chairs with his name printed on the back, a pair of sunglasses perched on top of his head.

"Now, remember," Mel continued, "Thursday, downstairs at the theatre. Be on time, and wear comfortable clothes. 'Bye now."

"Wait!" Gwen yelled into the phone but it was too late. All she heard was a dial tone. The stage manager hung up before she'd had a chance to ask her if the rest of the gang had made it into the play.

Gwen hung up the phone and turned to see her older brother Danny leaning against the doorsill, with his arms crossed and a superior smile on his face. He was tall and skinny as a rake, with black, slicked-back hair and square, dark-framed glasses. Danny spent most of his time at the library and looked just like what he was, the senior class brain.

"How long have you been standing there?" Gwen demanded.

"Long enough to witness your entire performance." Danny shook his head. He imitated her pretending to call herself and running in place by the phone. "That was the dumbest thing I've ever seen."

Normally her brother's needling got to her, but not today. Gwen looked him straight in the eye and said airily, "That performance, plus my superior musical talents, has just won me a part at the Carousel Dinner Theatre." She added casually, "I'll be co-starring with Nicholas Blade."

"Nicholas Blade?" Her brother dropped his arms to his side, a startled look on his face.

"That's right," Gwen replied, reaching for another cookie. "You remember him, don't you? The famous TV star?"

Danny squinted at her suspiciously. "You're kidding." Then he added, less confidently, "Aren't you?"

Gwen shrugged nonchalantly. "Show up on opening night, and we'll see who's kidding."

From the dazzled look on her brother's face, she could tell that he was not just impressed, but *very* impressed. This was Gwen's moment of triumph and she knew it. "Maybe, if you're nice, I can get an autograph for you."

Before he could say a word, Gwen swept grandly through the living room and into her bedroom. As soon as she had shut the door behind her, and she knew no one could see her, Gwen jumped up and down in a circle, hugging herself and squealing, "I got it! I got it!"

Just as quickly, she stopped. "What if I'm the only one of us in the play?" Gwen murmured out loud. "I'll have to be singing and dancing with complete strangers on a stage in front of hundreds of people." She shuddered at the thought. "That would be awful!" Gwen snatched up the pink Princess phone and quickly dialed a number.

"Reed residence, Zan speaking," a familiar soft voice answered.

Gwen got right to the point. "Zan, it's Gwen. I'm in the play. Are you?"

"Yes!" Zan shouted in her ear. "Mel just called to tell me. Isn't it truly wonderful?"

"Fantastic!" Gwen bellowed, not caring whether her brother heard her enthusiasm. "I was afraid I'd have to go it alone."

"I'm so glad you called. I was too nervous to phone you. I wonder if the rest of the gang made it in?"

"Hang up!" Gwen ordered. "And let's call them. You take Rocky, and I'll call McGee and Mary Bubnik."

The girls slammed down their phones without even saying good-bye. Zan flopped across the green-and-white quilt covering her brass bed and punched in Rocky's number. Although the rest of her parents' house was ultra modern, Zan had insisted on having an old-fashioned bedroom. Little white lace pillows were neatly arranged along the headbroad. She hugged one to her chest as she listened to the phone ring.

"Yeah?"

It was one of Rocky's brothers. Zan could hear the television playing at full volume in the background. "May I speak to Rocky, please?" she asked politely.

"Yo, Rocky. It's for you." Rocky's brother yelled so loudly that Zan had to hold the phone away from her ear.

"Who is it?" Zan heard Rocky shout back in the distance.

"Your friend," he bellowed

"Which one?"

"I didn't know you had more than one," her brother retorted.

"Ask who it is, Michael," Rocky shouted.

"Look, I'm not your secretary." There was a loud clunking sound as Michael dropped the phone to the floor. Zan heard pounding footsteps as Rocky's voice shouted, "What did you do that for, you jerk?"

"My arm was getting tired," Michael drawled.

Before Rocky could get into a shouting match with her brother, Zan yelled, "Rocky, it's Zan. Pick up the phone."

"Zan? Sorry about Michael. He's a total slime, but I was trying to watch *Nicholas Blade, Private Eye*."

45

"Is it on now?" Zan said, checking the slim gold watch on her wrist.

"Yeah, they just rolled the opening titles. Now they're showing some dumb deodorant commercial so we have a minute to talk."

"I just wanted to see if you got cast in *The King and I.*"

"Sure," Rocky replied. "And so did everybody else."

"Even Mary Bubnik?"

"Yeah. I guess not being able to sing on-key or walk straight didn't matter."

"How did you find out?"

"I asked. Hey, Nick's back on. Catch you later."

Zan winced as Rocky banged her phone down on its hook. She stared at the receiver and shook her head. "Doesn't anyone say good-bye anymore?"

Gwen called McGee and the two girls didn't say a word, they just squealed for a full minute. Then Gwen said, "I have to call Mary Bubnik. I'll talk to you later."

When Mary Bubnik heard the good news she shouted, "I just can't believe it! Me and Nicholas Blade together on the same stage, in the same theatre, singing the same songs—"

"Hopefully in the same key," Gwen murmured under her breath.

Mary didn't hear her remark but continued, "My mom is so excited, she's already talking about buying me some new outfits."

46

Gwen stuck her hand in the cookie jar, then stopped. "I'm starting a whole new diet just for Nicholas," she announced dramaticaly. "I'm cutting out Twinkies completely."

Mary was suitably impressed. Twinkies were Gwen's favorite food. The two girls talked about what they would wear to the first rehearsal, and what they would say to Nicholas Blade when they first met him.

Suddenly Mary Bubnik giggled. "I just thought of something."

"What?"

"Now that we're all in the play, it's not *The King and I* anymore."

"What is it, then?"

"The King and *Us*!"

Chapter Five

The following Saturday the gang couldn't wait to get to ballet class so they could show off in front of the Bunheads. They were the first ones in the studio and positioned themselves at the *barre*, eagerly watching the door. Each of them had taken special care with her appearance that morning. Even McGee had put on a new pair of tights. "Look, Ma," she announced, holding her leg up for the others to see. "No holes."

"I wish you would quit sticking your feet in my face," Gwen grumbled. "Save it for the Bunheads."

"Speaking of *them*," Rocky said, "how are we going to break our good news to them?"

"Why don't we come right out and tell them?" Mary Bubnik suggested, blinking her big blue eyes.

"That wouldn't be any fun," McGee objected. Her eyes twinkled with mischief. "I think we should break it to them slowly so we can watch them die of jealousy."

They all giggled wickedly, then stopped as the door banged open and Courtney flounced into the studio. She was talking to Page, who was right behind her, and didn't even notice the gang warming up in the corner.

"Can you believe that Nicholas Blade is actually in Deerfield?" Courtney breathed excitedly. "He's one of my absolute favorite TV stars."

"Me, too," Page agreed. "Sometimes when I watch his show, I pretend he's rescuing me, and not Suzanne Childers."

"I do, too," Courtney giggled. "Then I pretend that we get married, and have a TV show of our very own."

"How *sweet*," Rocky called sarcastically from the corner.

Courtney spun to face them, a horrified look on her face. "How long have you been there, eavesdropping?"

"We were here first," Gwen shot back. "You're the ones eavesdropping, not us."

"But you weren't saying anything," Page observed.

Mary Bubnik grasped the *barre* and did a *grand plié*. "That's because we were warming up. We have to be in shape for our big dance numbers."

"That's right," Zan said, placing her foot on the *barre* and bending over to touch her forehead to her knee. "With all the TV producers and reporters out in the audience, we'll truly want to do our best."

Gwen tried to imitate Zan's movement but she couldn't get her foot onto the *barre*. With a loud thunk it slammed to the floor. She pretended like she had done it on purpose, kicking her leg into the air and slamming it down on the floor again and again. "There will probably be a lot of talent scouts there, too," she declared, "looking for fresh new faces."

Page Tuttle put her hands on her hips. "What talent scouts?"

Courtney narrowed her eyes at the group. "What audience?"

"All the people who will be coming to the Carousel Dinner Theatre to see our show," Zan said proudly.

"And our *star*," Mary Bubnik added.

"Star?" Courtney repeated sarcastically. "And what show might that be?"

The girls couldn't contain themselves any longer and they shouted as one, "*The King and I*, starring Nicholas Blade, Private Eye!"

"What?" Courtney and Page shrieked in dismay. "Are you in that?"

Gwen shrugged her shoulders. "Of course."

"But — but how could that happen?" Courtney stammered. "We never knew . . ."

"There was an audition notice on the bulletin

50

board last week," Rocky said innocently. "Didn't you see it?"

Courtney crossed her arms angrily. "No, we certainly did *not*."

"I wonder why," Zan replied. "Miss Delacorte posted it right after class."

"Oh, that's right," McGee said, snapping her fingers. "You guys were meeting with Mr. Anton about serving cheese and crackers at the gala."

Page cocked her head in confusion. "But we came back into the dressing room right after that, and I didn't see any notice."

Rocky shrugged. "Maybe you just forgot to look at the board."

"Or maybe somebody took it off the board, so we'd never get a chance to see it." Courtney stared hard at the gang.

It took every ounce of willpower for the girls to keep a straight face and look innocent. "Do you think so?" Zan said, her voice dripping with concern. "That would be just too awful."

"Rotten is the word for it," Page said, glaring at them. "Really rotten."

"I'm going to talk to my mother about this," Courtney declared, moving swiftly toward the door. "She'll get us a part in that play."

McGee groaned. "She's not on the board of the Carousel Dinner Theatre, too, is she?"

"No," Courtney admitted. "But she's got influence."

"Well, you can try," Rocky said matter-of-factly, "but I don't think it'll work. You see, the play is all cast. Mel, the stage manager, told me so when she called." She added brightly, "Say, maybe you could be our understudies."

"I — I'd rather die," Courtney sputtered.

"What roles are you playing?" Page asked.

"Nicholas Blade's children," Mary Bubnik said proudly.

Courtney raised her eyebrow. "*All* of you are playing his children?"

"Well, I guess he had a lot of kids," Mary Bubnik replied.

"You guess?" Courtney sniffed her disapproval. "Don't you even know the story of the show?"

"Well, um . . ." Mary Bubnik didn't want to admit that she actually knew nothing about it. She turned to McGee, who gave a helpless shrug. She'd never even heard of *The King and I* until the day Miss Delacorte had tacked the notice on the board.

"Of course, we know the story," Rocky declared confidently. "It's about this king who had all these children and, uh, he liked to sing a lot." She figured that was a safe assumption to make because, after all, the show *was* a musical.

"And?" Courtney demanded.

Rocky hesitated. "And, uh . . ." She turned to Gwen and said blithely, "You fill in the details."

Gwen had seen *The King and I* on the late-night

movie once, but she'd been too young to remember anything about it now. "Well . . . um . . ."

Finally Zan, who loved the show, came to the rescue. "The King of Siam hires an English governess named Anna to tutor his children. But she ends up teaching him, too, and there are all of these romantic and funny scenes. Especially the ballroom one, where she teaches him to dance."

Mary Bubnik giggled. "It sounds wonderful."

"It is." Zan's eyes shone with excitement. "And it is also tragically sad because the King falls in love with Anna, and she with him, but because he's the King of Siam, and she's a foreigner, they really can't get together. And the best and most romantic part of all is —" Zan clasped her hands to her chest. "It's a true story."

"Whoever gets to play Anna and fall in love with Nicholas Blade is lucky," Page Tuttle said wistfully.

Courtney sighed right along with the rest of them. "Really lucky."

"Well, we'll be working with Nicholas Blade, Private Eye, every day," McGee informed them.

Rocky smiled and added, "Maybe we can get an autograph for you."

"Oh, would you?" Page gushed.

Courtney elbowed her. "I'm sure Mummy can get his autograph just as easily."

"But she won't be with him every day," Page protested. "I mean, they're going to be playing his children."

"Right," Courtney said. "All because they pulled a dirty trick."

"You don't have any proof of that," McGee retorted.

"Well, I'm going to call my mother anyway," Courtney said, flouncing out of the room. "You won't get away with this." Reluctantly Page followed her out the door.

Once they were alone, the girls burst into laughter. McGee was grinning so hard, her cheeks ached. "Can you believe it? The Bunheads are jealous!"

"I don't blame them," Mary Bubnik said. "Not only are we going to be in a musical at the Carousel Dinner theatre but —"

"But!" Gwen took a deep breath. "We're going to be starring with the most handsome hunk in the whole wide world!"

The gang raised their voices in triumph.

"Nicholas Blade, Private Eye!"

Chapter Six

When McGee entered the green room at the Carousel Dinner Theatre on the following Tuesday evening wearing a floral print dress, her four friends gaped in amazement.

"What are *you* doing in a dress?" Gwen demanded in disbelief. McGee never wore a dress if she could help it. Gwen gestured to the others who were in jeans and sweatshirts. "Mel told us to wear comfortable clothes."

"This dress is very comfortable," McGee replied, crossing her fingers behind her back. Actually, the puffed sleeves cut into her arm, the waist was too tight, and the big red scab on her knee from baseball practice stuck out like a neon sign beneath the hem of her skirt. But McGee didn't care. She was bound and determined to have Brett notice her as a girl this time, not as a baseball player.

"Besides," McGee added, "I thought I should look nice for our first rehearsal."

Before Gwen could reply, they were distracted by the sound of arguing voices from the corner of the room.

"If we have too much gold in the opening number, we'll never be able to top it in the embassy scene," the costumer named Cheryl insisted as she poured herself a cup of coffee. She wore an apron covered in safety pins and had a tape measure draped around her neck. "Too much gold lamé is going to look tacky."

Her partner Monty shook his head emphatically. "Remember, this play *is* set in Thailand." He held up his hands in a helpless gesture. "I mean, everything is glitz for days."

"Hello, everyone!" The girl with the waist-length blonde hair strolled into the green room, followed by one of her friends. She had an oversize nylon bag looped over her shoulder and was talking in an even louder voice than during the auditions.

"Look who made it into the show," Gwen whispered to the gang.

"When Mel called me, I nearly died," the girl exclaimed. "I mean, even though I *have* done four shows here, I get just as excited as if it were the first." She noticed the costumers in the corner and waved furiously. "Hi, Cheryl, Monty, we're back!"

"Congrats, Ashley and Dawn!" Monty said, coming up beside her. "Wait till you see your costumes, they're fabulous."

Ashley tossed her silky hair, which shimmered and rolled about her waist like a pony's tail. She was totally aware that everyone was watching her.

Her friend, Dawn, with the black hair and glasses, told Monty, "I can't wait to work with our director. I've always wanted to be in a Hayden Wilson show."

"Take it from me," Ashley declared, "Hayden's the best but . . ." She lowered her voice to a loud whisper. "He can be a real terror if he thinks you're goofing off. He won't put up with any joking around, believe me."

Moments later two more girls dressed in fluorescent pink leotards and black bicycle shorts flounced into the lounge. They spotted Ashley and squealed, "You made it, too?"

"Was there ever any doubt?" Ashley gestured for them to join her and her friend around the couch. Pretty soon all of the chairs were taken by Ashley and her pals, who chatted together gaily.

Zan turned to her friends and said in a shaky voice, "They all act like they've been doing this forever."

"That's the secret," Rocky replied. "They're *acting*." She jerked her thumb at one of the girls who'd just come in. "At the audition I heard that short girl in the pink top tell her mother that she'd never even *seen* a play before."

57

"I bet down inside they're as nervous as we are," Mary Bubnik said.

Gwen pushed her glasses up on her nose. "Maybe we should act like we know what we're doing and then we'll feel better."

"Right." McGee tugged at the waistband of her dress and squared her shoulders. "Let's get something to drink."

The five of them moved in a tight cluster to the refreshment table where a cooler of lemonade had been set beside the coffeepot, along with a basket of cookies.

Mary Bubnik set a paper cup beneath the lemonade tap and pressed it on. "This is really exciting," she babbled to no one in particular. "When we did *The Nutcracker* with the Deerfield Ballet, they wouldn't let us have food backstage. We couldn't even get a glass of water." As she talked Mary kept her hand on the tap and didn't even notice that her cup was overflowing.

"Mary, look out!" McGee shouted as the lemonade gushed over the edge of the paper cup and down onto Rocky's red high-top sneakers. Rocky leaped out of the way to the side, bumping Mary's elbow, and the whole glass spilled out onto the black-and-white linoleum floor.

"Oh, gosh," Mary Bubnik said with a high-pitched giggle, "everyone's going to think I'm a real klutz."

"Think?" Gwen rolled her eyes toward the ceiling.

58

"I guess I'm just a little nervous about meeting Nicholas Blade, Private Eye," Mary Bubnik whispered. She held out her hand. "Look, my hands are shaking."

"I'm nervous, too," Zan whispered. "I dreamt about him all night." She sighed and patted Mary on the arm. "We'll just find a mop and clean this mess up." She turned around in a circle, looking for the broom closet. "I wonder where they keep it?"

"Why don't you ask the janitor?" Gwen suggested, pointing to a plump, balding man in a gray one-piece jumpsuit leaning against the far wall. "Maybe he'll even clean it up for you."

"Excuse me." Mary Bubnik tapped the man on the shoulder. "Could you tell me where the mop is? I spilled my lemonade."

The man peered at her over the newspaper he was reading. "I haven't the foggiest idea where they keep those things," he said crisply. "Why don't you ask the custodian?"

Mary was startled to hear that he spoke with a rich British accent. "Aren't you him?"

"Me? Heavens, no! I'm in the play."

"You are?" Mary Bubnik smiled at him. "That's great. So am I. Who do you play, the grandfather?"

"What!" The man glared at her as he slapped the newspaper against his leg. "For your information, there isn't a grandfather in this play. Now go bother someone else." He flipped the newspaper up in front of his face.

Mary was taken aback by his angry response. Rocky grabbed her arm and whispered loudly, "Don't mind him, Mary, he's probably just upset 'cause he got a small part and he has to move scenery."

"Move *scenery*?" The man dropped the paper again and glared at Rocky indignantly. "Young lady, don't you know who I am?"

The five girls stared at him, trying to remember if they had ever seen him before.

Gwen looked him up and down carefully. "Where would we have seen you?"

"On your television," he retorted.

"You've been on TV?" Mary Bubnik perked up at that information.

McGee snapped her fingers. "I got it. You play the old man in that commercial where no one sends you any mail and you look sad and finally one of your kids calls you, right?"

Rocky punched her on the arm. "No, he doesn't. He's the old guy on that ad for prunes."

"That's it." Gwen imitated an old man bent over a cane and holding up a prune toward an imaginary camera. "By cracky, these are good," she said, mimicking an old codger's voice.

"Grandfather? Old man? Prunes?" the man repeated, his face getting redder and redder. He tossed his newspaper on the coffee table and commanded, "Come with me!"

They didn't budge, and he added, "*Now!*"

"We better go," Rocky whispered, "just to calm him down."

McGee nodded. "If we don't, the old coot might give himself a heart attack."

The man marched them down the hall into the theatre lobby, where several framed photographs had been hung around a large poster advertising the show. He tapped on the glass covering one of the pictures. "Who do you think that is?"

"That's Nicholas Blade, Private Eye, of course," Zan replied with a heartfelt sigh.

"Now who do *I* look like?" The man stood beside the photo and smiled.

"The man in the prune commercial," Gwen answered matter-of-factly.

"No!" He slapped his forehead and muttered, "I can't believe this. Are you *completely* dense?"

He stared at them for a full five seconds, then back at the glossy portrait of the famous actor.

The gang stared at him curiously.

"Well?" he asked hopefully.

They shook their heads slowly.

The man heaved a large sigh, then struck another pose, smiling and winking over his right shoulder, and giving the thumbs-up sign with his left hand.

Rocky was the first to realize who he was. Her jaw dropped open and she said in a choked voice, "I— I don't believe it!"

The man folded his arms and glared at her. "Believe it, young lady."

"What's he talking about?" McGee asked.

"That's . . ." Rocky sputtered. "I mean, this is . . ."

"Who?" Gwen demanded.

"Nicholas Blade, Private Eye."

"What?" The other four stared at the man in shock.

"You — you *can't* be," Mary Bubnik gasped. "You're old, and bald —" Mary clapped her hand over her mouth as she realized how awful her words must have sounded.

The man winced at her words. "And you, my dear, are young and rude."

Rocky tried to come to Mary's rescue. "What she means, is . . ." Her voice trailed away as she struggled for the words to describe how they felt. "Nicholas Blade, Private Eye looks much different. He has hair. See?" She pointed at the picture of a tanned young man with a full head of blond hair. "He's handsome and is a super hunk." She eyed the man's bulging midriff suspiciously. "But you're . . ."

"You've made your point," the actor said, hurriedly cutting her off. He starred at the promotional picture and shook his head in frustration. "I told my agent we shouldn't use this photo anymore, but she insisted. Said my public expected to see Nicholas Blade, Private Eye."

"But how can you look like *that* on TV? McGee pointed to the poster and then back to him. "And like *this* now?"

The actor threw up his hands in frustration. "Haven't you ever heard of reruns? I shot that series almost twenty years ago."

"Twenty years ago?" Mary Bubnik gulped. "We weren't even alive then."

"Frankly, my dear, I'm surprised you've lived this long," Nicholas Blade remarked acidly. Then he threw open the lobby doors and strode back into the theatre.

The gang stood in speechless amazement. Zan finally broke the silence. "I can't believe that's Nicholas Blade, Private Eye." She stared glumly at the photo behind the glass. "He was my hero. I just can't believe it."

Gwen shoved her glasses up on her nose. "I can't believe *you* guys. You all amaze me."

"What do you mean?" McGee tossed the baseball that she carried with her everywhere, over and over again. "What did we do?"

Gwen ticked off the list on her fingers. "You just told a major TV star that he was old, fat, and bald."

"Well, we were in shock," Mary said in self-defense. "We didn't say it on purpose."

Gwen shook her head. "Nicholas Blade is going to hate you forever."

"Gwen's right," Zan gasped. "He'll probably never speak to us again. I'm so embarrassed."

"Wow, this is awful!" Rocky slumped against the brick wall. "I promised everyone in my homeroom I'd get them Nicholas Blade's autograph."

"And I told my mother I'd introduce her to him,"

Mary said. "I don't think I'll ever be able to face him."

"You're going to have to." Gwen tapped her watch with her finger. "Because rehearsal starts in three minutes."

Mary looked horrified. "We can't go in there — not after what we said."

"Well, what do you suggest we do?" Gwen asked.

"Quit," Rocky declared. "That's the only way out."

The five of them pondered that thought in silence.

"What are you doing in the lobby?" a warm male voice broke in from behind them. "Aren't you supposed to be in rehearsal?"

They sprang apart in alarm and McGee lost her balance, crashing right into the stranger's chest. When she looked up, she found herself looking into Brett Allen's eyes.

"Whoa, take it easy," he cried, reaching out to steady her.

At the touch of his hand, McGee shot back like she'd been stung. "Oh, um... hi, Brett," she stammered, wondering if she looked as foolish as she felt. "We were just, you know — thinking."

"Sounds serious," Brett said with a wink. Then he noticed the baseball she was clutching in her hand. A quizzical frown creased his forehead. "Are you sure you don't play with the Fairview Red Sox?"

McGee hurriedly put the ball behind her back. "Positive. I don't even like sports."

"That's too bad." Brett shrugged. Then he pretended to tip an imaginary hat. "See you inside."

As soon as he was out of sight, McGee declared, "Well, it's obvious that we have to stay in the show."

Rocky looked at McGee like she'd lost her mind. "What do you mean, obvious?"

McGee didn't want to admit that she was developing a major crush on Brett. But if they didn't stay with the show, she might never see him again, and that would be awful.

"We made a commitment," McGee said, breaking into the pep talk that her coach always gave to her team before a tough game. "And now we have to stick to it. The director cast us, and he's counting on us to come through for him. So we need to focus all of our energy on winning —"

"Winning?" Mary Bubnik cocked her head.

"Sure I mean winning." McGee emphasized her words by hitting her hand with her fist. "We're battling the Bunheads, remember? And for the first time in a long, long while, it looks like we really might win."

McGee's speech was starting to get Rocky fired up. "McGee's right," she said, her dark eyes flashing. "I say we get into that rehearsal and give it our best shot."

"But what do we do when we see Nicholas Blade again?" Mary Bubnik asked nervously.

Rocky gulped. "Duck."

Chapter Seven

As the girls entered the auditorium, the stage manager handed them each a manila envelope. Then Mel ordered, "All children of the King, onstage for the 'Getting to Know You' number."

"What's that?" Mary Bubnik hissed as they trotted down the aisle toward the stage. "Do we introduce ourselves?"

"No," Zan explained. "It's one of the musical numbers."

A young man in front of them turned and said, "You'll find the words inside your packet. Also, there's a name tag in there. Put them on when you get a chance."

"Speaking of names," Rocky said, "what's yours?"

The young man grinned. "I'm Emmet, the A.S.M."

"A.S.M?" Mary repeated.

"Assistant stage manager," Emmet replied. "That's another word for go-fer. If you need any help, just holler."

The girls hurriedly pulled their name tags out of their packets and stuck them on their shirts. Halfway down the aisle they passed Brett Allen, who was chatting with another actor.

"Prince Chulalongcorn, you're in this number," Emmet called. "Onstage, please."

"He plays a prince?" Mary Bubnik repeated, obviously impressed.

The blonde girl named Ashley was walking in front of Mary. She rolled her eyes at her friend, Dawn, and called over her shoulder, "Well, of course. That's what you call the King's children. We're all princes and princesses."

"We are?" Mary Bubnik turned to Rocky. "Boy, won't the Bunheads be envious? I mean, they're playing royal ring bearers but we're actual royalty!"

Rocky cracked a half smile and murmured, "That's pretty cool."

McGee could hardly contain the butterflies forming in her stomach. She was going to be in a scene with Brett!

Emmet stopped to talk to the accompanist, while Ashley and Dawn led the rest of the children up the steps to the stage. McGee looked around her and took a mental head count of their group. There were fifteen boys and girls present, ranging in age from about four to eighteen.

"Kids, listen up!" the director, Hayden Wilson, shouted as he took his place in front of them. "We've got a lot of work to do, and very little time to do it in. Today, you're going to learn the song, and the movements that go with it. Then we'll block in Anna and the King."

"Block in?" Gwen raised an eyebrow.

Rocky whispered out of the corner of her mouth, "That's where they tell the actors where to move on the stage."

"You mean, Nicholas Blade, Private Eye, is in this scene?" Mary Bubnik asked. She had hoped she wouldn't see him anymore that day.

"Well, it *is* called *The King and I*," Dawn replied. "I have a feeling he's probably in most of the play."

"Now if I could have your attention!" Hayden Wilson glared at them impatiently. "I'd like to introduce Nickie Feddersen, our choreographer. She will teach you the movements. I'll be back in one hour to see how you're doing."

Nickie, a perky girl with curly, sunstreaked hair pulled back in a ponytail, bounded out in front of them. She wore a gray-and-pink striped leotard with pink leg warmers and a pink striped headband. "Okay, is everybody ready?"

Several kids cheered. The four-year-old just looked shy and embarrassed.

"Okay! Now I'm going to put you in four different rows." As she talked Nickie pointed to places where she wanted people to kneel. "Of course, the Prince should be in the first row along with the featured dancers."

Brett knelt down in the first row. Ashley flipped her hair off her shoulder and knelt beside him.

Nickie clapped her hands together. "Okay. The littlest members should also be up in front, so the audience can see you." Several of the younger kids scooted forward.

"I'd rather sit in the back," Mary Bubnik whispered. "That way, if I forget my steps, I can watch other people."

"Me, too." Zan, who suffered from awful stage fright, had already positioned herself near the curtain lining the back of the stage. The rest of the gang fell in beside her and the choreographer seemed to go along with the arrangement.

Nickie knelt down in front of the entire group and slapped her hands on her thighs. "Johnny will play the music, and I'll show you the movements, okay?" She didn't wait for an answer but cocked her head and giggled. "Okay!"

The accompanist pounded through the music while some of the children stumbled through the words to "Getting to Know You." Nickie waved first her right hand, then her left. She nodded her head over each shoulder, then pretended to shake hands with someone in front of her, and then to someone on each side. She did that several times, then stood up and spun in a circle repeating the gestures. When she finished she called out, "Okay, everybody got it?"

"Is she for real?" Gwen grumbled. She had been busy trying to find the sheet music in her packet and had completely missed the entire demonstration.

Ashley raised her hand and leaned to the side so her hair swept the floor beside Brett. "I've got it, Nickie," she said breathlessly.

"All right, Ashley!" Nickie clapped her hands together enthusiastically.

"Nod, clap, wave, stand, shake, shake, shake," Rocky mumbled, trying to remember the correct sequence.

Zan shook her head. "I think it's nod, *wave*, clap, stand, shake, shake, shake."

"I don't remember a clap being in it," McGee said, scratching her head.

"That's the only thing I *do* remember about it," Mary Bubnik said, pursing her lips. "It's those nods and shakes that have me all messed up."

Nickie hopped off the stage, conferred with Johnny Ogden at the piano for a moment, then scurried back up the steps. "Okay, kids. Let's try to stumble through it and see where we are, okay?"

"If she says one more *okay*," Rocky muttered, "I think I'll scream."

70

"I bet she was a cheerleader in high school," Mary Bubnik whispered. "She's awfully perky."

"*Too* perky, if you ask me," Gwen remarked sourly. Girls who looked that good in leotards and smiled all the time irritated her.

"She's just trying to get us excited about our parts," Mary Bubnik countered.

While Gwen and Mary Bubnik talked, Johnny played the tune again and this time several more girls joined in on the verse. When the music stopped Mary Bubnik gasped, "Oh, shoot! I was so busy talking, I completely missed the practice."

Nickie clapped her hands together enthusiastically. "I think we're at a place were we can bring the director back. It looks like most of you have it." She skipped off into the wings of the theatre, calling over her shoulder, "I'll be right back, okay?"

"No, it's not okay," Gwen shouted after her. "I don't know my nods from my shakes."

"Well, you should have paid attention, instead of talking so much," Ashley said, turning around and glaring at Gwen. "That's just not done in the theatre."

Gwen could feel everyone staring at her and her face started to heat up. She folded her arms across her chest defensively. "What makes *you* such an authority? One production of *Alice in Wonderland*? Big deal."

"Frankly I don't know how *that* group got in the show," Ashley said loudly to the first row of children around her and Brett in particular. "Anybody can see they don't have any experience, and some of them are just downright awful."

Just then Hayden Wilson the director returned. Two other people were with him.

"Look!" McGee whispered. "There's Nicholas Blade, Private Eye."

"He still looks old," Gwen responded grumpily.

"That must be the woman playing Anna," Zan whispered. "She's beautiful."

A tall, slender woman wearing a blue silk blouse that showed off her clear blue eyes smiled at all of them. She was obviously dressed for rehearsal because she wore a hoop skirt and ballet slippers. Her dark hair was piled loosely on the top of her head, and she had a pencil tucked behind one ear.

"Cast," the director said, gesturing grandly toward the two actors, "may I present Nicholas Blade and Deborah Gregg — our King and Anna."

Brett led the rest of the King's children in hearty applause. One tiny girl crawled forward and pulled at Nicholas Blade's pant leg. "May I have your autograph, please?"

The gang watched the actor smile warmly and say, "Why, certainly, my dear. I'm flattered."

"Gee, he's acting completely different with her," Mary Bubnik whispered. "He seems almost nice. I wonder what happened?"

"Think about it," Gwen whispered back. "I mean,

how would you feel if someone told *you* you were old and bald?"

"Hmmm." Mary Bubnik sat back on her heels. "You've got a point."

"What do you have to show us, Nickie?" the director asked.

"Well, the dance is kind of rough," Nickie replied, "but I think most of the kids have it." She knelt back down on the floor. "So, gang, let's do it. Okay?" She gestured to Johnny, who hit a chord on the piano.

"Wait," Zan complained, "I'm not ready."

"Ready or not," McGee whispered, "here we go."

Mary Bubnik kept her eyes glued to Ashley and tried to mimic her movements. So did the rest of the gang. That worked fine while they were kneeling but once it came time to stand up and turn, they got totally confused. Then the woman playing Anna started singing along with them and that really threw them off.

She smiled patiently as Mary and Gwen bumped into each other, but kept right on singing.

The collision threw the whole row off and they wound up being exactly two moves behind the rest of the ensemble.

"Stop! Stop the music!" the director shouted above all of the singing. Once the accompanist stopped playing, Hayden Wilson put his hands on his hips and demanded, "What are you doing back there?"

Gwen and the others turned to look behind them. All they saw was a black curtain.

"I'm talking to you five," the director snapped, "in the back row."

"Us?" They all gulped at once. They could feel a lecture coming on.

"Yes, you. You all seem to be waving and shaking your hands but it has nothing to do with what Nickie taught you. Weren't you paying attention?"

Ashley turned around and smirked at Gwen.

Brett had also turned around to stare, and McGee wanted to sink into the floor. "He's looking right at me," she groaned.

"No, he's not," Gwen disagreed. "He's staring at me."

"Who are you talking about?" McGee demanded.

"The director," Gwen replied.

"Oh, who cares about him?" McGee said, with a wave of her hand. "It's Brett I'm worried about."

"Well, you'd better worry about the director," Rocky cut in. " 'Cause he's coming this way."

Hayden Wilson strode up and down in front of them, his arms folded tightly across his chest. "I cast you girls because you told me you were from the Deerfield Academy of Dance."

"We are," Zan said meekly.

"You certainly don't move like it."

"Well, that's because we were concentrating on the words to the song," Rocky explained hurriedly. "We got a little confused."

74

"Humph!" The director marched back to the front of the stage. "Well, from now on, pay attention to the steps. We open in seven days, for heaven's sake."

He flopped down onto a folding chair that Emmet had placed on the stage for him. "Okay, let's put Anna and the King into the scene." Mr. Wilson pointed at Brett. "We'll start from your line."

Brett stood up and folded his arms defiantly across his chest. " 'I do not believe such thing as snow,' " he began, quoting the words from the script.

"He's good," McGee murmured softly.

"Well done, Brett!" The director sprang out of his chair. "Now, kids, after Brett says this line, I want you to form a circle around Anna and all jump up and down and scream, 'Me, either.' Then when the King comes in, I want you to be silent and drop to your knees with your heads bowed. Got that?" He stared meaningfully at the gang.

"Got it," Rocky called confidently.

"Good." The director flopped back in his chair. "Brett, do your line again."

Brett stood up and did them even more forcefully than before.

"He just gets better and better," McGee murmured to herself.

"Okay, kids!" The director leaned forward in his chair intently. "Scream!"

Suddenly the air rang with the cries of fifteen high-pitched voices.

"*What* is going on here?" The King's voice echoed

75

across the theatre as he entered the scene. Instantly they dropped to their knees as the director had told them to do. Rocky and Mary and Zan fell right at the King's feet.

Anna gave her next line and waited for the King's reply. He stood there for thirty seconds with his mouth open but nothing came out. Finally the actor shook his head. "I'm sorry, Hayden, I'm going to need my script for this one. For the life of me, I can't remember my next line."

"That's quite all right, Nick," the director replied, a thin smile plastered on his face. "Opening's still a week away."

"Thanks." Nicholas Blade pulled a dog-eared script out of his back pocket and slipped a pair of reading glasses onto his nose. Zan, who still couldn't get over how old her hero had become, gasped when he put on his glasses.

"Not only is he fat and bald," Rocky whispered, "but he's also blind."

Nicholas Blade was just about to read from his script when he overheard Rocky's remark. "I'm sorry, Hayden, but this is impossible!" the actor exploded angrily. "Do I have to be this close to the children?" He glared at the gang. "It's hard for me to concentrate."

"Move wherever you want to, Nick," the director replied impatiently. "Just give us your lines — please."

Nicholas read his part from his script and than

the director slapped his hands together. "All right, that's it for today. I'll see you all back here tomorrow night, same time, and I want this dance *perfect*. Good night, all."

There was an eruption of sound as the crowd on stage broke up and scattered across the auditorium.

"Perfect?" Mary Bubnik squeaked nervously, as she followed the others back toward the lobby. "I've never done *anything* perfect."

"Don't worry," Rocky said, punching her on the shoulder. "I'll teach you the movements."

"In the meantime," Gwen said with a grin, "I told my mom to pick us up at Hi Lo's after rehearsal. I knew we'd be starved from all the hard work."

"What hard work?" McGee demanded. "All we did was sit on the floor, wave our arms around, shake hands, and get yelled at."

"Right," Gwen said. "Getting yelled at always makes me hungry. Come on!"

Chapter Eight

"Hey, wait up!" a voice called from behind them as the gang stepped through the lobby doors into the cool evening outside.

Mary Bubnik looked over her shoulder, then spun around and squealed, "It's Brett! I think he wants to talk to us."

"Brett?" The girls stopped in their tracks.

Mary Bubnik quickly patted her blonde curls into place. "How do I look?"

"Chill out, Mary," Rocky hissed. "You look fine."

Gwen slipped her wire-rimmed glasses into her back pocket and tried to suck in her stomach. "I wish I hadn't eaten that Twinkie before rehearsal," she groaned.

Zan, who towered over most boys her age,

slumped her shoulders to make herself shorter. "I wonder what he wants to talk to us about," she mumbled without moving her lips.

"I don't think he wants to talk to *us* about anything," Rocky remarked as Brett walked straight up to McGee.

"Mel said your name is Kathryn. Is that right?" he asked with a friendly smile.

"That's my name," McGee said, "but you can call me by my nickname —" She paused suddenly. She didn't want to tell him her nickname was McGee. That sounded so unfeminine. McGee bit her lip, trying to think of something. "Um, Katie."

"Katie," Brett repeated slowly, as if he were savoring the word. "That's nice."

Mary Bubnik, who was standing right next to McGee asked innocently, "Who calls you that?"

McGee turned to Mary and said between clenched teeth, "Everyone."

"I didn't know that — oomph!"

A sharp jab in the ribs from Rocky and a stomp on the toe from Gwen stopped Mary Bubnik in mid-sentence.

"Ow!" Mary clutched her side and hopped up and down on one foot. "Why'd you do that?"

"Because," Rocky hissed between clenched teeth as Zan and Gwen grabbed Mary Bubnik by the arm and pulled her away from McGee and Brett.

McGee covered her face with her hand. "I can't believe those guys some times," she mumbled, completely embarrassed. Finally she turned to Brett and asked, "What did you want to ask me?"

"I was wondering if you happened to catch the Reds game last night on TV," Brett replied.

"Oh, yeah, what a disaster, huh?" McGee shook her head and chuckled. "I mean, you can't commit three errors in one inning and expect to win."

"They looked like they were asleep out there," Brett said, nodding in agreement.

"More like they were in a coma," McGee cracked.

Brett burst out laughing, then added, "And how about that Grotowski, walking four batters in a row?"

"He's had a really weird season so far," McGee said, coming to the pitcher's defense. "But when he's hot, no one can touch him. Look at last week when he pitched that no-hitter against the Mets."

McGee stopped talking when she realized that Brett was grinning at her slyly. "What's the matter?"

"I thought you said you didn't like sports."

Her green eyes widened. She'd completely forgotten she'd told him that. "I don't," McGee covered quickly, "but my dad does. He forces the whole family to watch every game."

Brett nodded. "Does you father force you to play them, too?"

McGee had already told Brett that she wasn't on the Fairview Red Sox. He'd almost caught her in one lie already. She realized she had to stick with her story, no matter what. "No, I don't play sports," McGee declared firmly. "That's for guys. I like ballet and, uh . . ." She racked her brain trying to come up with something that sounded really feminine. "Knitting."

Gwen guffawed behind her, while the rest of the gang snickered loudly. McGee wanted to sink right into the earth. "Um, listen, Brett," she blurted out, "I really have to go now. I'll see you at the next rehearsal, okay?" Then she turned and raced past her friends down the sidewalk.

"Hey, McGee!" Rocky shouted. "Wait for us!"

She ignored their cries and ducked around the corner out of sight. When the gang finally caught up, McGee turned on them in a fury.

"You guys are complete, total slime! How could you do that to me? Brett's going to think I'm a jerk."

"What's he going to think when he finds out you're a liar?" Gwen countered.

McGee put her hands on her hips. "What lie?"

"Aw, come on — *Katie*," Rocky said mockingly. "You told Brett you didn't like sports, and that you were a ballerina who knits. I'd call that a major lie."

"Well, it's sort of true," McGee retorted. "I mean, I don't like *all* sports — I hate golf, you know. And I have taken ballet for years."

"What about the knitting?" Rocky countered.

McGee squeezed one eye shut and squinted at the gang. "Okay, that was a lie."

"I don't understand why you don't want him to know you like sports," Mary Bubnik said.

"Because!" McGee threw her hands up in frustration. "Don't you see? He'll think I'm just another jock and start treating me like all the other guys I know."

"But what if he finds out the truth?" Zan asked.

"The only way he'll find out," McGee replied, "is if *somebody* tells him."

She shot a dark look at Mary Bubnik, who said quickly, "Don't look at me. I won't tell."

"Come on, McGee, it won't work," Gwen said, shaking her head. "You'll never get away with it."

"Sure I will," McGee insisted. "Look, you guys, I only have two more league games left this season. And then I won't be lying anymore. But you've got to help me out, okay? Please?"

The pleading look in McGee's eyes was impossible to resist. The gang looked at each other and nodded.

"Okay," Zan said. "We'll do whatever we can."

"But when it blows up in your face." Gwen added, "don't say we didn't warn you."

"Thanks, you guys," McGee said with a grin. She gestured toward the familiar red-and-white awning above Hi Lo's restaurant. "Let's get a soda, or something."

Gwen's eyes lit up. "Perhaps a small order of fries, with ketchup and onions. All this tension makes me hungry."

Rocky stared at Gwen in amazement. "Is there anything that *doesn't* make you hungry?"

Gwen considered this for a moment. Finally she simply said, "No."

Hi Lo was in the kitchen when they walked into

his place. He stuck his head out the serving window and shouted, "Eureka! I've got it!"

"What have you got?" Gwen called as the gang clambered up onto the stools lining the counter.

"My latest special," the old man replied proudly. "And you five are just in time to be the first customers to try it."

"Whoopee," Rocky muttered under her breath. "Lucky us."

Mary Bubnik frowned nervously. "It wouldn't happen to be anything like the last one, would it?"

"That one was dangerous," Rocky observed.

"Yeah," Gwen cracked. "That exploded in your face — *not* in your hand."

"Oh, no, this one is very safe," Hi reassured them, chuckling merrily. "There's not an ounce of baking soda in it."

In a flash Hi burst through the swinging door carrying his big silver platter. Sitting in the center was a bizarre object that resembled a giant pink pretzel. He set the tray on the counter and said, "Ta-da!"

"Wow. That certainly is... colorful," Gwen said, trying to think of something nice to say about it. "What do you call it?"

"Hi Lo's Incredible Strawberry Twist." He picked up a knife. "Now, who wants the first bite?"

Each of them pointed to the girl beside her, crying, "She does!"

"Ah." Hi nodded sagely. "I see that you are all a bit wary of what might be inside, am I right?"

83

The girls all bobbed their heads up and down.

"Then why don't I be the first to taste it?" Hi suggested. "Then you will see that my latest special is perfectly safe."

"I think that's a great idea," Gwen declared. "And if you survive, you can tell us how it tasted."

"Thank you for that vote of confidence," Hi said with a chuckle. "Here we go." With a flourish he spun the knife in his hand and pressed it against the dough. The girls tensed for the worst but nothing happened. "Hmmm," Hi murmured, stroking his chin. "Maybe I need a sharper knife."

While Hi rummaged in a drawer at the end of the counter, Mary Bubnik reached out her hand and knocked on the pastry shell. It thunked loudly.

"Did you hear that?" she whispered.

Zan nodded. "I think he's going to need something sharper than a knife."

"Like a chain saw," Gwen drawled.

"Here we go." Hi returned with a large meat cleaver. He raised his hand over his head and slammed the metal into the dough. The pink pretzel flipped up in the air.

"Duck!" McGee shouted as it hit the salt and pepper set in front of them. The saltshaker shattered from the force of the collision, and the solid pretzel dropped onto the floor behind them.

"Geez Louise!" McGee exclaimed. "That sounded like a bowling ball hitting the floor."

"It *feels* like a bowling ball," Rocky remarked as

she picked up the pretzel. She hefted it in her hands and looked at the shopkeeper in amazement. "This thing weighs a ton. What did you put in it, Hi?

"One of my secret ingredients," Hi replied, shaking his head. "It was supposed to give it some weight."

"It sure did that," Gwen agreed. "And turned an innocent-looking pretzel into a deadly weapon." She looked up at Hi and cracked, "Have you thought of going into the spy business?"

"That would be great," Zan giggled. "Exploding pastries and two-hundred-pound pretzels."

Hi dropped the pretzel back on the tray and studied it for a moment. Finally he said, "I'd better go see where I went wrong before I forget the recipe." He disappeared back into the kitchen, leaving his failed creation on the counter in front of them.

"If you ask me," Mary said in a hushed voice, "I think Hi would be better off forgetting that particular recipe."

The girls were still giggling when the bell tinkled over the door and Courtney's voice sang out behind them, "Well, look who's here!"

Rocky dropped her face in her hands and groaned, "Oh, no, it's the queen of the Bunheads."

"We just finished our rehearsal for *Sleeping Beauty*," Courtney announced, "and I'm simply exhausted."

"I guess standing there holding that pillow can really take a lot out of you," McGee quipped.

"Very funny," Courtney sniffed. "For your information, we do a lot more than just stand on the stage."

"I'm practically heartbroken we won't be able to see you," Gwen said sweetly, "but, as you know, we'll be performing those particular nights in *The King and I* with Nicholas Blade, Private Eye."

"I was talking to my mother about that," Courtney said with a condescending smile. "Someone in the know told her that rehearsals are going really poorly."

"Oh?" McGee said carefully.

"Supposedly poor Nicholas Blade can't remember his lines because he's gotten so old." She clucked her tongue and added, "They're predicting the show will be the biggest bomb ever."

"Well, your mother heard wrong," Rocky retorted. "Nicholas Blade is *not* old. In fact, he looks exactly like he does on TV."

Mary Bubnik crossed her fingers behind her back and declared, "Why, he's more handsome than ever."

"It must be all the weight lifting he does," Zan chimed in, "that keeps him so young-looking."

"Young-looking? A *bald* guy?"

"Well, of course, he's bald," Zan replied. "But that's just for the production. Everyone knows that when you play the King in *The King and I*, you shave your head. Yul Brynner did it in the movie and won an Oscar for his performance. Now it's a tradition."

Courtney was unruffled. "Well, even if he *does* have hair — which I doubt — Mother said that he can barely remember his lines."

"He doesn't have to know his lines until opening night," Gwen said calmly. "You see, Courtney, this is a musical, not just an ordinary play." She spoke slowly and carefully, as if she were talking to a baby. "Nick's concentrating on his singing and dancing first, because they're more difficult. Then he'll learn his lines."

The edge of Courtney's eye twitched slightly. Then she spun around and slammed her fist on the counter. "May I have some service, *please!*"

Hi popped his head out the serving window from the kitchen. "Certainly." The old man bustled through the swinging door, wiping the flour off his hands with his apron. Hi picked up his green pad and looked up expectantly. "Now what can I get you?"

"Certainly not *that*," Courtney said, pointing at the huge pink pretzel that sat on the counter. She stared at it suspiciously. "What is it, anyway?"

"That's my Hi Lo Strawberry Twist," Hi said. "It has several secret ingredients inside."

Courtney's lip curled slightly. "I'll bet it does."

"Why don't you try it, Courtney?" Gwen suggested, trying to keep a straight face. Then she whispered to Rocky under her breath, "It'll break her teeth off."

"I'm on a diet." Courtney said with extra emphasis to Gwen. "That looks a little too heavy."

"You can say that again." Rocky giggled.

"Just make me a banana yogurt shake," Courtney declared. She looked at the one remaining stool at the counter and sniffed. "To go. I'll wait by the cash register."

Hi nodded and disappeared into the kitchen.

"I can't believe you guys," McGee hissed as Courtney walked out of hearing range. "You tell me not to lie, and then you turn around and tell the biggest whopper I've ever heard."

"But we had no choice," Mary Bubnik insisted.

"Besides, the Bunheads will never find out," Rocky said as Hi brought Courtney her shake. "They're in *Sleeping Beauty* and won't be able to come see our show."

Courtney paid for her shake and as she pushed open the door, she called back over her shoulder, "Oh, by the way, Mother got us tickets for your opening night."

"What?" McGee gasped. She spun around on her stool and stammered, "D-d-don't you have to do the ballet?"

"We're off that night."

As she went out the door, Courtney's parting words sent a cold stab of fear into the hearts of five stunned girls.

"Just remember... I'll be watching you!"

Chapter Nine

On Wednesday afternoon, McGee's Little League team was scheduled to play the Thunderjets at the municipal ballpark in downtown Deerfield. Zan, Gwen, Rocky, and Mary Bubnik joined the large crowd of parents and friends that had gathered to watch the rival teams battle for first place in the league standings.

"Since we have to go straight to rehearsal, Mom packed us a light supper," Gwen announced as the gang took their places on the bleachers behind home plate. She patted the red-and-white cooler on the bench beside her. "And I added my own personal touch. Turkey sandwiches, Cokes, caramel popcorn, celery stuffed with cream cheese and walnuts, corn chips, ice-cream bars, chocolate-chip cookies, and a bag of M&M's."

"All of that is for supper?" Mary Bubnik asked, wide-eyed.

Gwen chuckled. "Of course not. The celery sticks are the hors d'oeuvres before lunch, the sandwiches, chips and Cokes are lunch, the ice cream and cookies are the dessert, and the M&M's and popcorn are just snacks — in case we get hungry later on."

Zan clutched her stomach. "Just hearing your list makes me feel stuffed."

"Not me." Gwen flipped up the lid of the cooler. "It makes me hungry." She held up a celery stick. "Anybody for an hors d'oeuvre?"

Mary Bubnik and Zan shook their heads. Rocky wasn't paying attention. She had brought her father's binoculars so they could get closer looks at the players. Right now she was scanning the crowd.

"Uh-oh," Rocky announced, training the binoculars on the parking lot. "We've got trouble at two o'clock." She used the military language her father had taught her to describe the location.

"Let me see." Mary Bubnik pulled the binoculars out of Rocky's hands and tried to put them up to her eyes. Unfortunately the strap was still wrapped around Rocky's neck.

"Stop!" Rocky said in a stangled voice. "You're choking me!"

Mary just leaned in closer, keeping her eyes firmly

glued to the eyepiece. "Oh, my gosh, you're right," she gasped. "There's Brett Allen."

"If Brett sees McGee playing baseball," Rocky said, "he'll know she lied to him and think she's a big phony."

Zan's eyes gew huge. "We've got to warn McGee."

Gwen took a loud bite of her celery. "Well, we can't go to the dugout."

"Why not?" Mary Bubnik asked, getting to her feet. "The game hasn't started yet."

"If we go to the dugout, Brett will see us and know we're here to watch McGee."

"That'll give her away just as badly," Rocky agreed.

"I've got an idea," Zan said excitedly. "Once, when Tiffany Truenote was trying to signal someone in a crowd, she used a mirror. If you catch the sunlight at the right angle, you can aim it just like a spotlight."

"Good idea," Rocky said. "We'll signal McGee and have her meet us underneath the bleachers."

"Only one problem," Gwen said, reaching into the cooler for another celery stick. "Where are we going to get a mirror?"

Rocky bit her lip. She never wore any makeup and Zan hadn't brought her purse along.

"I used to have one," Mary Bubnik said, rummaging through her purse. "But I think I lost it along with my pen and my wallet."

"If you don't have a pen or a wallet," Rocky asked curiously, "then what's in your purse?"

"Let me see." Mary held up a wadded-up pink tissue. "Some Kleenex, a whole bunch of gum wrappers, the cover to my pen that I lost, two bottle tops, and the ticket stub from the movie we went to last month."

"All trash." Rocky shook her head in astonishment. "That's amazing. You are wearing a pink leather garbage bag."

Zan had been watching quietly as Gwen methodically devoured all of the "hors d'oeuvres." When Gwen started munching on the caramel popcorn, Zan snapped her fingers. "I've got it. Hand me that plate, will you?"

"Which plate?" Gwen replied with a full mouth.

"The aluminum one that's holding the sandwiches."

Gwen shut the lid. "That's our supper," she protested. "We should at least wait for the game to start."

"Wait?" Rocky arched an eyebrow. "I didn't notice you waiting. Aren't those the 'end-of-the-game-just-in-case-we-get-hungry' snacks you're eating?"

"Maybe." Gwen hurriedly tried to gulp down the evidence. "But that doesn't mean —"

"I don't want the sandwich," Zan cut in impatiently. "I just want the plate. We can use it for our mirror."

"Oh." A broad smile burst out on Gwen's face. "In that case, here." She handed the plate to Zan, who quickly tried to catch the sunlight on its shiny surface.

"It's all in the angle," Zan murmured. "Rocky, tell me if the coast is clear."

Rocky took the binoculars back from Mary Bubnik and searched the crowd. "Brett's in the bleachers on the Thunderjets' side." Then she turned in her seat. "And McGee is warming up on the grass behind her team's dugout." She dropped the glasses and nodded. "All clear."

McGee was standing beside other members of her team with her feet apart, waving her arms like a windmill as she bent over and touched each foot with the opposite hand.

Zan tried to reflect the light into McGee's face, but without success. "She's bouncing up and down too much."

"Here, let me try." Gwen grabbed the plate to give it a try but only succeeded in shining the light into the eyes of the boy warming up next to McGee. When the beam hit him he winced and covered his face.

"Oh, great," Rocky muttered. "Now you've blinded the pitcher."

"Well?" Gwen snapped. "Can you do any better?"

"Sure." Rocky set her binoculars on her lap and cupped her hands around her mouth. "Yo, McGee!"

"Rocky!" Mary Bubnik squeaked. "Brett might have heard you."

"I'm sure he didn't, and even if he did, he thinks her name is Katie."

At the sound of her name McGee squinted toward the bleachers. Gwen caught her attention and motioned for her to meet them. They watched as McGee nodded and, tucking her glove under her arm, jogged off the field right toward them.

"Quick, head her off at the pass!" Gwen shouted.

Rocky climbed over the railing and sprang off the side of the bleachers, landing directly in McGee's path.

"What's going on?" McGee asked.

"In here." Rocky grabbed McGee's baseball jersey and yanked her under the bleachers. "Quick."

"Hey, cut it out," McGee protested. "My game starts in a few minutes."

"Forget the game," Rocky said. "You've got a problem that's spelled B-R-E-T-T."

"Brett?" McGee tried to sound casual. "What about him?"

"He's here."

"What?" McGee felt her heart pound in her chest. "Where?"

"He's sitting over by the Thunderjets' dugout."

McGee took off her baseball cap and rubbed her sleeve across her forehead. "This is terrible. Do you think he's seen me?"

Rocky shook her head. "But he will, as soon as you hit the field."

"Oh, golly." McGee slumped against one of the bleacher supports. "What should I do?" McGee looked back at her dugout nervously. "I can't pretend I'm sick. Coach has already seen me warm up."

94

Rocky scratched her head. "Maybe you should just tell Brett the truth."

"I can't." McGee shook her head violently. "That would be too embarrassing."

Rocky shrugged. "Well, don't you think you'll be pretty embarrassed when Brett finds out you lied to him?"

"You're right." McGee paced back and forth underneath the bleachers. "But if I tell him I lied, then I'll have to tell him why."

"Why *did* you lie to him?"

"Because ..." McGee hesitated, then admitted softly, "Because I like him."

Rocky nodded brusquely. "You're right, that *would* be totally awful — telling a guy you like him." She took a stick of chewing gum out of her jacket pocket, unwrapped it, and popped it in her mouth. "We're going to have to think of something else."

McGee kicked at the dust with the toe of her cleats. "I wish this game weren't so important, and I could send someone out there to play for me." His eyes widened suddenly. "Do you think ... ?"

Rocky contemplated taking McGee's place for only a second. "Naw," she said reluctantly. "My specialty is karate. I can't play baseball; I'd ruin the game."

McGee sighed heavily. "Yeah, it was a dumb idea." She slapped her cap back on her head and one of her braids got pulled up beneath it.

"Wait a minute," Rocky said, noticing the hidden braid. "Maybe it wasn't such a dumb idea after all." She reached out and tucked McGee's other braid under her hat. "Maybe we could make you *look* like someone else."

"Just by tucking my hair under my hat? Get real."

"Now hold on." Rocky circled McGee. "We can make a few other changes, too." She rubbed her chin thoughtfully. "It's too bad we don't have a pair of sunglasses."

"How about regular glasses?" a voice called from above them.

Rocky and McGee looked up and realized that Zan, Gwen, and Mary Bubnik had been watching them through the slats of the bleachers.

"Gwen wears glasses," Mary Bubnik continued. "McGee could wear those."

"What am I supposed to see with?" Gwen asked, turning her head.

"You don't have to see," Rocky answered. "Now toss them down here."

Gwen removed her wire-rimmed glasses reluctantly. "Listen, if you break these, my mother will kill me." She squinted at McGee. "Do you promise to take good care of them?"

Rocky rolled her eyes. "She promises. Now, hurry up, the game will be over before you make up your mind."

Gwen carefully dropped her glasses through the narrow opening between the floorboards, and

McGee caught them in her glove. Rocky took them and slipped them on McGee's face. "There! You look completely different."

"So do you." McGee blinked behind the thick lenses. "You're all blurry. How am I supposed to play ball?"

Rocky slid the glasses down to the tip of McGee's nose. "Like that. Just look over the top."

"Humph." McGee wasn't convinced.

"Um, Rocky?" Zan called softly from above their heads. "I think we might possibly have another problem."

"What?" Rocky put her hands on her hips and looked up.

"Look." Zan reached her arm through the opening and pointed at the back of McGee's baseball jersey. Printed in big red letters was her last name.

"Oh, no," Mary Bubnik cried.

"Hey, don't worry about it," Rocky said, dismissing the problem with a wave of the hand. "Gwen? Toss me down one of those sodas."

Gwen reached into the cooler and pulled out an ice-cold Coke. "What are you going to do with it?" she asked as she dropped it down.

"Watch." Rocky caught the can and popped open the lid. To Gwen's horror, she poured the drink out onto the dirt.

"Why did you waste that?" Gwen protested. "That was brand new."

"Relax." Rocky knelt in the dirt and swirled the

mess into a gooey mass of mud. Then she scooped up a handful and slapped it on McGee's back.

"Oh, gross!" McGee said as the cool, wet mud hit her shoulders. "I hope that washes out."

"Don't worry, it will." Rocky kept smearing the mud around until her name was totally obscured. Then she slapped some on McGee's legs and down the front of her shirt. "This way it will look like you slid into home."

"*Before* the game has started?" McGee objected.

"Hey, what do you want?" Rocky shot back. "I'm creating a disguise, and I don't have much to work with here."

"McGee, your team is in a huddle around your coach," Mary Bubnik called out. "Does that mean something?"

"It sure does." McGee peered up at the blurry figure above her. "It means I'm late."

"One more thing." Rocky whipped off her red satin jacket and stuffed it inside McGee's shirt around her waist.

"What are you doing?" McGee cried, slapping at her hands. "Cut that out!"

"This is to make you look heavier." Rocky examined her handiwork one more time, then nodded with satisfaction. "Good. Your own mother wouldn't recognize you." She pressed McGee's glove back into her hand and pointed her toward the field. "Now get out there and win!"

When McGee reached the dugout she turned and gave the thumbs-up sign to her friends in the bleachers. She felt confident that her team would win and the disguise would work.

And it would have, too, if Tony "Macaroni" Marconi, the pitcher for the Thunderjets, hadn't thrown McGee a wild curve on his first pitch. It hit her square in the stomach.

One moment McGee was standing at the plate with her bat in the air, and the next moment she was on the ground, listening to voices coming from behind the backstop.

"It looked just like she exploded," one woman said in a nasal voice. "First her braids flew out of her hat —"

"Then her glasses fell off," a deep-voiced man added.

"Then it looked like she lost ten pounds on the spot," a little girl giggled. "That was incredible."

McGee squinted one eye open to see if what they were saying was true. Rocky's jacket lay on the ground beside her. Next to it were her cap and Gwen's glasses. And next to the glasses were a pair of Reebok tennis shoes that belonged to —

"Brett!" McGee bolted to her feet. "Gee, I uh, didn't know you were here. What a surprise."

Brett crossed his arms and stared at her. "I'm the one who's surprised. I thought you didn't play sports. You said you didn't even like them."

"I didn't—I mean, I don't," McGee stammered, trying hard to look everywhere but at him. "At least, not all of them."

"Boy, are we glad to see you back on your feet," Mary Bubnik broke in as she and Gwen lugged the cooler up beside the backstop.

"No kidding, McGee," Rocky said, dusting off her jacket. "For a second there, when that ball hit you in the stomach, we really thought you were hurt. I guess my jacket cushioned the blow."

"McGee?" Brett cocked his head. "I thought you said your friends all called you Katie."

"My goodness, nobody calls her *that!*" Mary Bubnik replied, trying to be helpful. "She hates it with a passion." She giggled and leaned toward Brett confidentially. "Take my advice—don't *ever* call her that."

McGee didn't think it was humanly possible for her to feel any more embarrassed than she did at that moment. She was wrong.

"Where are my glasses?" Gwen dropped her end of the cooler to the ground and put her hands on her hips. "If you've broken them, McGee, you'll have to pay for them. I'm not kidding."

"Geez Louise, Gwen, not now," McGee muttered.

"These belong to you?" The umpire dangled a pair of wire-rimmed glasses in front of Gwen's face. The frames were bent and the right earpiece was completely gone.

"Oh, that's just great, McGee," Gwen said angrily.

"Now I'm going to walk around blind just because you wanted to play baseball in disguise."

"Disguise?" Brett shook his head in confusion. "What for?" As McGee turned back to face him, he asked, "And why did you lie to me?"

Before she could answer, the umpire took her by the arm. "If you can walk, you're going to have to clear the field. We have a game to play."

McGee felt little beads of sweat form all across her forehead. Everyone seemed to be shouting at her at once, but all she could hear was a loud roaring in her ears.

"McGee!" her coach shouted from the side. "I want you back in the dugout. Let's hustle."

"All right!" she shouted back angrily. "I'm trying to, but people keep blocking my way."

Unfortunately for McGee, she directed the last words right into Brett's face. He stepped back with exaggerated politeness. "Ex-cuuuse *me!* Who wants to hang around a liar, anyway?"

With that Brett spun on his heel and marched off the field. McGee watched him go and felt her eyes blur with tears.

"Come on, McGee," Rocky said, grabbing her arm. "He's just a dumb boy. What does he know?"

"Yeah," Zan added. "Forget about him."

"How can I forget about him?" McGee wailed. "I have to see him in rehearsal in less then two hours."

Chapter Ten

When the girls arrived at the theatre that evening they were fifteen minutes late. Mel, the stage manager, met them at the stage door with her clipboard in her hand, a stopwatch around her neck, and an angry look on her face.

"You've just broken the first rule of the theatre," she growled. "Never, but *never* be late. Especially to a dress rehearsal."

"I'm sorry, Mel," Rocky said, "but it wasn't all of our faults." She scowled at Gwen. "*She* wanted to stop at the store."

"Well, I had to refill the cooler," Gwen protested. "It was completely empty because *you* spilled the last Coke on the ground." Then she glared at McGee and added, "And I had to get some masking tape for my glasses since *somebody* broke them."

"Look, it wasn't my idea to wear your stupid glasses," McGee retorted. She crossed her arms and glowered at Mary Bubnik.

"Okay, okay, the glasses were my idea," Mary Bubnik said with a sigh. "But you don't have to get so touchy about it. I mean, if you hadn't have stepped in front of that baseball, the game would have ended a whole lot sooner, and we would have been here on time."

"Stepped in *front?*" McGee couldn't believe her ears. "The pitcher threw a curve ball low and inside. I never had a chance to get out of the way."

"Yeah, sure," Rocky scoffed. "Tell me another one."

"Stop it," Mel snapped, pressing her fingers against her temples. "I don't need this. Not tonight. Just don't be late again. Monty!" She motioned to the makeup man, who was busy pinning a sarong onto a palace guard. "Take over. Please."

Monty hurried over to them, the tape measure draped around his neck flapping in the air. A row of safety pins were fastened up and down the length of his white smock. "All of you are in dressing room four." He clapped his hands briskly. "Now get a move on. Cheryl will bring you your costumes. We're going without makeup tonight so don't worry about putting any on. Just get in there and get dressed. We want you on the stage in five minutes."

"Good grief, this is ridiculous!" Nicholas Blade's voice thundered from inside dressing room number one. He appeared in the center of the hall, wearing a pair of gold lamé breeches that barely reached his knees, and a red sash wrapped around his waist. His chest was bare.

"It's the King!" Mary Bubnik cried. Then she covered her mouth and tried not to giggle. "What a weird outfit."

"Monty, old boy, may I speak with you a moment?" Nicholas smiled stiffly as he pointed to his pants. "You don't really expect me to appear in public looking like *this,* do you? These look like a pair of girl's bloomers."

Monty hurried to his side. "We knew the pants were too short, Mr. Blade, but we just wanted to see you in them to see what else we needed to change."

"Well, you can start by changing everything," Nicholas replied, struggling to keep his voice calm. "My entire wardrobe is dreadful."

"What's the matter with his chest?" Zan whispered loudly. "It looks like he sat out in the sun and got a burn on only one side."

The actor's eyes widened as he recognized the gang. "For your information," he said between clenched teeth, "this miserable excuse of a theatre has run out of body makeup." Then he turned and snapped at Monty, "Or am I *supposed* to play the King of Siam as a two-tone?"

"Now, Mr. Blade, please try and relax," Monty said

104

soothingly as he ripped open the seam of the pants and safety-pinned it back together. "Everything will be right as rain before the night is over."

"It had better be," Nicholas Blade said, turning red in the face. "Because I'm not going out on that stage and have these — these *girls* giggling at me behind my back!"

Monty spun to face the gang. "What are you still doing here? I told you to get dressed. Now do it!" He bellowed the last sentence and the gang jumped to obey.

"Boy," Zan muttered as the girls raced into their dressing room, "everybody is a real grouch today."

Their dressing room was long and uncomfortably narrow. A counter stretched the length of one wall, and a mirror lined with globe lights was above it. A rack of costumes extended along the other side. There was barely enough room for them to squeeze into their places in front of the makeup mirror.

Mary Bubnik grabbed one of the costumes off the rack and held it up in front of her. "These look like boys' pajamas," she complained.

"They are," Zan replied, reading the label. "Red nylon pajamas from Penney's." She held up one of the sleeves. "Look. They've sewn gold braid all around the cuffs to make them look Oriental."

"And they took the buttons off the front," Rocky added, "and put snaps and embroidered ribbon down the middle."

"Gee, I thought we'd have something more fun

to wear than dumb old boy's P.J.'s," Mary Bubnik said, slumping down in her chair.

"You think that's bad?" McGee called. "Check out the headgear we have to wear." She stepped out from behind the door wearing a coiled black hairpiece on top of her head. Stapled to it was half a paper plate sprayed with gold paint. McGee made a face and declared, "Instant Bunhead."

Just then Mel stuck her head in the door. "Aren't you girls ready yet? You're supposed to be onstage for the 'Getting to Know You' number."

"No one's told us how to put our costumes on," Gwen replied.

"Well, figure it out. We're practicing the set change in and out of the scene so get dressed — *now*."

Mel's voice and face were taut with tension, and the gang realized she meant business. They sprang into action, grabbing the pajamas with their names pinned to them off the hangers.

"Quick." McGee tossed each of them one of the buns with a paper plate attached to it. "Stick one of these on your head."

All five of them faced the dressing room mirror and fastened the hairpieces to their hair. Then they raced down the corridor toward the stage and joined the other kids playing the King's children, who were standing in line quietly waiting to go on. The backstage area was lit by two red bulbs that gave everyone's face a ghostly glow.

"When is it our turn?" Rocky asked Ashley, who was standing in the wings watching the stage.

"They're going over another scene first," she replied. Then Ashley turned to look at the gang and choked. "Who did your hair?"

"We did." Rocky self-consciously touched her bun and asked, "What's the matter with it?"

Ashley rolled her eyes. "Well, you're supposed to tuck your hair *into* it — not wear it like a hat."

"We knew that," Gwen bluffed. "We were just in a hurry. Don't worry, we'll do it right when we have an audience."

Ashley made a clucking sound with her tongue. "You'd better." She turned her back on them to watch the action onstage.

"Do you see Brett?" McGee whispered over her shoulder as they took their places in line.

Ashley spun around and, putting her fingers to her lips, said in an exaggerated whisper, "*Shhhh!* He's acting." She pointed to the stage and they saw that Brett was playing a scene with the King.

"I wish we could get a better look," McGee whispered.

"We can." Rocky pointed to a ladder running up the side of the black wall to a small platform above the stage. "If we climbed up there, we'd have a perfect shot of him."

"But aren't we supposed to do our song next?" Mary Bubnik asked.

"Sure." Rocky was already halfway up the ladder. "But we can't do it till this scene is over," she called softly over her shoulder. "We'll have plenty of time to get back down."

McGee and the rest of the gang followed her up the ladder to a tiny wooden platform anchored to the wall. Ropes were draped across it and they had to duck their heads to keep from hitting their headpieces on them. They huddled together and peered down through the lighting instruments to the stage floor below.

Gwen was still without her glasses and she grumbled, "What am I doing up here? I can't see."

"I can't look," Zan whimpered, covering her eyes with her palms. "I'm afraid of heights."

Gwen watched the stage for a moment and then batted herself on the ear. "I must be going deaf, too. I can't hear a thing."

"That's because it's the King's turn to speak," Mary Bubnik replied. "And he can't remember what he's supposed to say."

"Uh-oh," Rocky whispered. "That's what Courtney said would happen."

They listened to the King clear his throat several times. Finally he shook his head and stared out at the audience. "I'm sorry, the words have gone right out of my head. Can someone give me my line?"

The girls heard Mel's voice echo over the intercom, "The line is, 'Someday *you* will be King.' "

"May I remind you, Nick," the director called out

from the audience in an exasperated tone, "that opening night is only two days away?"

"I'm fully aware of that," Nicholas Blade shot back. "I just had a slight memory lapse."

"Slight?" They heard the director mutter to an assistant, "He's been doing this all day."

"Wow!" McGee whistled low. "Brett looks great in his costume."

Zan uncovered her eyes for a second. "What's he wearing?"

"Well, he's got on long pants like the kind Nicholas Blade had on, and no shirt — "

"Does he have any muscles?" Gwen interrupted.

"Of course," McGee whispered. "He's wearing a black-and-gold vest and I can't quite see what he's got on his head." Grabbing hold of a rope that had been looped across the platform, she leaned out to get a better look. Suddenly it broke loose from the brick wall and McGee swung off the platform into the darkness.

"Yikes!" she squealed.

The gang watched in amazement as the wall behind Nicholas Blade and Brett that was painted to look like the inside of the King's palace suddenly flew up in the air. Standing behind it were several technicians with hammers. They looked up in startled surprise at the equally stunned actors.

"That rope is attached to the backdrop," Rocky gasped. "Her weight is changing the scenery. Hold on, McGee!"

"Heads up!" one of the workers shouted as he fell backward, trying to avoid the wall swaying above him. Unfortunately his fall propelled him into another piece of scenery and his hammer burst clear through the painted canvas.

"Help me!" McGee yelled as she dangled precariously above the stage, swinging first to one side, then the other. She kept kicking her legs out, trying to get a foothold on anything that came near.

"McGee!" Rocky shouted, trying to snatch the rope as she swung by. "Don't kick like that, you'll hit the —"

"Too late!" Mary Bubnik wailed. She watched as a tall pillar wobbled back and forth and then toppled over toward the stage. "Timber!"

Rocky realized where the heavy prop was going to land and screamed, "Mr. Blade, get out of the way!"

The actor, who had remained in his position on the couch, looked up in alarm. His eyes widened and he leaped forward out of the way just in the nick of time.

With a deafening crash, the pillar landed squarely on the red velvet couch. Its legs broke off and ricocheted off into the wings of the theatre.

"Wow, it's smashed to smithereens!" Mary Bubnik gasped. Then she covered her mouth and pointed. On its way down, the pillar had caught the column standing on the other side of the stage, and now it was wobbling dangerously.

All of the King's children started screaming at the top of their lungs and fighting to get out of the way.

"Get me out of here!" one boy cried.

"It's an earthquake!" another girl shouted. "Help!"

The youngest just stood where she was and cried, "I want my mommy!"

Meanwhile McGee's rope was jerking her closer and closer down to the floor. The men on stage didn't realize she was the cause of the backdrop's sudden flight and several of them grabbed hold of its bottom edge and pulled.

"Whoa — what's happening!" McGee shrieked as she was suddenly yanked back up in the air. She sailed past the platform straight up toward the iron grid at the ceiling of the theatre.

"Oh, no!" Rocky shouted. "McGee's going to hit the roof!" Without thinking Rocky leaped off the platform and grabbed the rope with both hands. The addition of her weight slowed McGee's ascent.

"Come on, you guys," Rocky bellowed to the others, "we need more weight to bring her down."

Zan and Mary Bubnik looked to Gwen, who sputtered. "No way! I'm not jumping out there. I flunked rope climbing in gym. I can't even *see* the rope. Besides, it would probably break, and then we'd all die."

While Gwen babbled on, Mary Bubnik warbled, "It's now or never." She took a deep breath and leaped at the rope, shouting, "Here goes nothing!"

"How can they expect me to jump into the darkness like that?" Gwen muttered.

"Come on, we can pull from the floor." Zan scrambled back down the ladder without even thinking about being scared of the height.

"The floor?" Gwen repeated. "That's more like it." As she followed Zan down, Gwen shouted up to the three girls dangling from the rope, "Don't worry, we'll save you!"

When Zan and Gwen ran onto the stage and grabbed the end of the rope, Mel's voice came booming over the intercom. "Joe! Milt! Let go of that flat!"

The two workmen who were pulling at the edge of the wall looked up in confusion.

"There are little girls on the counterweight system," Mel called. "Let go *now!*"

Both men released the flat and suddenly Mary Bubnik, Rocky, and McGee came rushing toward the floor. McGee caught hold of one of the black drapes bordering the stage in an attempt to break their fall but it tore loose from its batten, and all three of them landed on top of Gwen and Zan.

A hush fell over the theatre as everyone onstage and off froze, waiting for the girls to stir. Finally Gwen groaned from the bottom of the pile. "Am I dead?"

"No," Zan muttered. "But I'm sure we will be soon."

Then the entire theatre exploded in sound, as the cast and crew hurried forward to see if they were all right. The director's voice could be heard above all the others, bellowing, "This is a disaster. A total disaster!"

"Now, Hayden, calm down," the stage manager was saying as she tried to restore order in the theatre. "Take a few deep breaths and relax."

"Relax? *Relax?*" The director ran his fingers through his disheveled hair. "Those little maniacs have destroyed my set, and you're telling me to relax?"

Mel looked up at a glassed-in booth in the back of the theatre and shouted, "Jamie, give us some light."

Suddenly the backstage area was bathed in a bright white light.

"Are you okay?" one of the workmen asked the girls, who were still lying in a clump on the floor. They couldn't answer but lay paralyzed with fear as the director stormed up the aisle toward them.

"Let me at them!" Hayden Wilson shrieked, hopping onto the stage.

"It was an accident!" Gwen pleaded, squeezing her eyes shut.

"Do you have any idea what you've done?" he thundered, standing over them with his hands on his hips.

Mary Bubnik grabbed the curtain that lay on the floor next to them and covered her head. "Don't kill us, Mr. Wilson, we didn't mean it."

The director's face was bright red, and he was

113

huffing in and out. "I'm not going to kill you," he said in a pinched voice. "I'm going to go one better — I'm firing you."

The gang stared at him in stunned silence. "We're fired?" McGee repeated.

"Yes, *fired*." Then he pointed toward the exit and roared, "And I want you out of the theatre this instant."

"But Mr. —"

"Now!"

Then Hayden Wilson spun on his heel and stalked off. He called back over his shoulder, "Mel!"

The stage manager hurried after him. "Yes, Mr. Wilson?"

"I want to talk to the cast in the green room in five minutes to reschedule rehearsal while we repair the set."

"Yes, Mr. Wilson."

Slowly the rest of the company began to go back to their duties. The girls sat silently as the technicians started to clear away the debris from the shattered pillar. The cast members broke up into little groups, talking among themselves. No one looked at the gang.

Rocky pulled herself to her feet. "Come on, you guys." She tugged at Mary Bubnik and Gwen, who were having trouble untangling themselves from the rope and curtain.

As she stood up, McGee caught sight of Brett standing by himself in the wings. He was staring at her. A tight lump formed in her throat, and it was all she could do to keep from crying. She felt very wobbly in the knees, though whether it was from the fall, or from being publicly humiliated by the director in front of Brett, she couldn't tell.

"Come on, girls." Cheryl the costumer was suddenly at their side. She squeezed Mary Bubnik's shoulder gently and said, "Let's get you out of those costumes and see if anybody got hurt."

They followed her blindly off the stage and through the green room, with their heads cast down in shame. McGee felt as if she could feel everyone they passed staring back at them. Once the girls were safely in their dressing room, she shut the door and sank down onto the floor.

"I don't know about you guys," McGee whispered in a small, tired voice, "but this rates as the absolute worst day of my entire life."

Chapter Eleven

"My mom's not coming to pick us up for two more hours," Gwen said as the group stood glumly outside the Carousel Dinner Theatre. "What should we do till then?"

"Well, I don't want to wait here." McGee glanced nervously over her shoulder into the theatre lobby. "We might see Mr. Wilson, and I don't think I could take that."

Gwen had been in such a hurry to get out of the theatre that she'd left her cooler and snacks in the green room. She felt a small rumbling in her stomach. "I wonder if Hi Lo's place is still open. Maybe we can get something to eat — to cheer us up."

Mary Bubnik nodded. "That's a good idea. Be-

116

sides, I don't like standing around in the dark. It gives me the creeps." She shuddered and pulled her pink sweater tight around her.

Once they left the bright safety of the theatre entrance, the night seemed to swallow them up. The sidewalk was deserted and one or two solitary streetlights cast gloomy shadows along the locked storefronts.

"It *is* kind of creepy here at night," Gwen whispered, looking nervously over her shoulder.

At the corner they paused and peered down the street toward Hi Lo's restaurant. A light shone through the window.

"Looks like he's still there," Rocky declared. "Come on."

The girls huddled closer together as they walked quickly down the street toward the familiar awning. "It's important to stay together," Zan advised them, "and to not walk too close to the buildings."

"How come?" McGee asked.

"A mugger could be hiding in the shadows and reach out and grab you."

As Zan spoke a small gust of wind blew a paper bag across their path and all five girls screamed and clutched each other in a panic.

"Stay under the streetlights," Zan ordered, once they'd regained their composure. "Muggers are less likely to step into the light. And if they do, you might be able to identify them later in a lineup."

"How do you know all this?" Rocky wondered, keeping her hands balled up tightly in fists, ready for action.

"Tiffany Truenote." Zan reflexively patted her purse where she carried a copy of the teen detective's latest adventure. "Tiffany always follows those rules when she's working on a case and has to go into an unfamiliar part of town."

"But this is all familiar," Mary Bubnik objected, pointing down the street at the marble steps of Hillberry Hall. "I mean, there's Hillberry Hall, where the ballet studios are, and Hi's restaurant is right across the street, like always."

McGee shook her head uneasily. "It looks so different somehow."

"Dark, is what it looks like," Gwen snapped. Her stomach was rumbling loudly. "I hope we get to Hi's soon. I get really hungry when I'm scared."

Zan motioned her to be quiet. "Isn't that strange? The whole block is dark. Hardly any of the streetlights are working."

"Like it was blacked out," McGee added.

"As if some creature of darkness had cast his evil shadow across the entire city." Rocky intoned in her best scary voice.

"Don't talk like that!" Mary cried as Rocky laughed mischievously. "You're frightening me."

Just as they came up to the door, they saw Mr. Lo silhouetted behind the glass. He was holding a huge set of keys in his hand and was in the process of pulling down the shade.

"Hey, Hi, it's us!" McGee banged on the door. "Let us in."

Hi looked at them in surprise, then quickly released the shade and opened the door. "My goodness, what are you girls doing out this late?"

"We need food," Gwen replied, clutching her stomach. "We're desperate."

"We were hoping you were still open," Rocky added.

Hi put his hat back on the metal coatrack. "For you, my door is always open." He made a sweeping gesture into the room. "Come on in, please."

"Thanks, Hi," Zan said as the five girls hurried inside and climbed up onto their usual stools.

Hi moved behind the counter and folded his hands in front of him. "Now tell me, what are you five *really* doing out on a night like this?"

"We were thrown out of the theatre!" Rocky announced with a dramatic toss of her hair.

The old man's eyes grew wide with surprise. "Thrown out?"

Mary Bubnik sighed. "Just because we had a weensy accident with the set."

"What happened?" Hi asked.

"We destroyed it," Gwen replied glumly.

"The director was furious with us." Zan popped her elbows on the counter and cradled her chin in her hands. "He fired us from the play. It was truly humiliating."

"Oh, my, oh, my," Hi Lo murmured, rubbing his chin. "This is terrible news."

Rocky nodded. "The absolute pits."

"So now we have to wait over an hour for my mom to pick us up," Gwen finished. She smiled hopefully. "We thought maybe some food would cheer us up."

"Of course." Hi's face suddenly lit up. "I have just the thing — my latest special. It's sure to put a smile on your face."

"Is it a new recipe?" Rocky asked hesitantly.

"Brand new. Never been tried before." Hi pulled off his coat, hung it on a hook by the kitchen door, and slipped an apron over his head. "Mary, why don't you fix everyone a milk shake while I get it ready?"

Mary Bubnik smiled and nodded. Once, when she had needed some extra money for ballet lessons, she had worked as Hi's assistant for a short time. He had taught her how to run the soda fountain, mix milk shakes, and whip up ice cream sundaes. As he disappeared into the kitchen, she skipped behind the counter and lined up five paper cups in front of her.

"Do you mind if we play the jukebox?" Gwen called through the serving window.

"Be my guest," came the shouted reply.

McGee dug in her pocket. "Who's got a quarter?"

120

Rocky held up a coin. "Me. But I get to pick the songs."

"Fine with me." The three of them moved to the opposite side of the tiny restaurant and, leaning against the old fashioned Wurlitzer, punched in their selections.

Mary dropped some scoops of ice cream into a large metal cup and turned on the blender just as the music blasted out of the jukebox speakers. The little bell tinkled over the door, but only Zan heard it.

She spun on her stool to see who had come in and froze. Two men in black overcoats, with stocking caps pulled down over their ears, stood framed in the doorway. The taller of the two had a long face and a twitch in his right eye that made him look like he was winking at everyone. His partner was a round little man with a chubby red face. Zan noticed that he kept his right hand buried in his coat pocket.

"M-M-Mary," Zan stammered. "We have customers."

Mary Bubnik had her back turned while she finished putting long plastic spoons in the five cups. "I'm sorry, y'all," she called brightly over her shoulder, "but the restaurant is closed."

"It's a bunch of kids," the short round man said in surprise. "But, Leonard, they're not supposed to be here."

"I told you, don't call me by my real name," the tall, thin man hissed at him.

121

The shorter man blushed and said, "Sorry, Leonard — I mean, sir."

Leonard stepped up to the counter. "Where's the old man?"

Mary Bubnik pointed to the swinging door. "He's in the —"

"He's not here right now," Zan cut in. "He asked us to watch his place till he got back." She forced herself to stay calm, hoping that Hi had heard what was happening and called the police.

"You cover the back door," Leonard barked at his partner, "and I'll get the cash."

The pudgy fellow moved over to Gwen, Rocky, and McGee, who were still huddled around the blaring jukebox by the rear exit and hadn't noticed a thing. He nudged McGee on the arm and asked politely, "'Scuse me. Would you three move away from the door, please?"

"Hey, what is this?" Rocky demanded as she spun around.

Zan, who'd been watching the entire thing, managed to squeak, "I think it's a holdup."

"A holdup?" McGee gulped.

All three of them froze in their tracks.

"What should we do?" Gwen asked, barely moving her lips.

Zan slowly slid off the stool and joined her friends. "Well, in most of the TV shows I've seen the robbers ask the innocent bystanders to get down on the floor with their hands over their heads."

The short, chubby guy stared at Zan, then smiled pleasantly. "That's a good idea. Would you mind geting down on the ground?"

"Not at all." Gwen threw herself face down on the floor in a flash. Zan, Rocky, Mary Bubnik, and McGee were right behind her.

Once again the pudgy fellow smiled. "Thank you."

"Cut the gab, Duane, and get over here." The tall man pounded on the cash register. "I can't get this thing open."

Duane stopped in the middle of the room and pointed at his partner. "Hey, you did it, too."

"Did what?"

"Called me by my real name."

"I'll call you something else if you don't get over here in two seconds." The tall man rolled his eyes in frustration.

Rocky, who'd been the most reluctant to get down on the floor, muttered, "Wow, these guys are brain-dead."

"Shhh!" McGee hissed. "They might hear you."

The sound of a siren suddenly split the night air and Leonard yelled, "It's the cops." He yanked out the cash drawer, and nickels and quarters spilled onto the floor.

"Way to go, Leonard," Duane said pointing to the coins.

Leonard growled. "Get down here and help me pick this stuff up! We've got to get out of here!"

"But what do we do about these kids?" Duane asked.

Leonard scooped up handfuls of cash and jammed them into his pockets. "We take 'em with us if we have to."

"Oh, I don't care for that idea at all!" Mary Bubnik said, lifting her head up to complain. "My mom is expecting me home, and she'll be really upset."

Gwen yanked Mary Bubnik back down on the floor just as the front door burst open. A figure in a leather jacket and jeans came flying through the air. In a single leap he landed with his foot firmly planted in the back of the Duane's knees. The stubby man dropped to the floor with a yelp of pain.

Leonard looked up from the spilled cash and gasped, "Oh, my God, it can't be! It's —"

"Nicholas Blade, Private Eye!" Zan shouted triumphantly. "To the rescue!"

With his racy leather jacket Nicholas Blade looked like he'd stepped right off the screen of his old series. He flashed the girls his trademark thumbs-up sign and winked.

Duane struggled to get to his feet, and Rocky screamed, "Nick, look out!"

Nick grabbed the metal coatrack standing by the open door, swung it over his head, and pinned Duane to the floor. "Girls," he shouted, "hold him down."

"Right!" Rocky and Gwen grabbed one end of the

metal pole and Zan, Mary Bubnik, and McGee sat on the other. For good measure Gwen rested her full weight on Duane's back.

The sound of falling coins made them all look around. Quarters were streaming out of a hole in Leonard's coat pocket and rolling all over the floor as he tried to slip past them.

"I wouldn't do that if I were you," Nick said, coiling himself into a karate pose. "These hands are registered weapons, and I couldn't be responsible for the consequences."

"Here we are," Hi announced, carrying a tray as he came out of the kitchen. "Hi Lo's Special . . ." His voice trailed off as he saw what was happening. "What's going on here?"

Leonard decided to bolt for the back door.

"Stop him!" McGee shouted.

Nick sprang forward and grabbed the tray out of Hi's hands. He hurled it like a Frisbee and it caught Leonard in the back. There was a resounding clap of sound as Hi's special soufflé exploded whipped cream everywhere.

"All right, Sergeant Milligan!" Nick shouted over his shoulder in a deep baritone. "Bring in your men!"

There was a pause as everyone turned to look at the door. But nothing happened.

After a second Duane raised his head up from the floor. "I just remembered. Sergeant Milligan ain't no real person. He's from your TV show."

Nick held his ground, but chuckled nervously. "It was just a joke. A small joke."

Leonard wiped the whipped cream off his neck with his fingers. "I'm not laughing."

He clenched his hand in a fist and moved toward Nick just as two men in blue uniforms leaped through the front door. "Police! Nobody move."

Chapter Twelve

"Mr. Blade, you were spectacular!" Mary Bubnik cried.

The actor was leaning against the counter, trying to catch his breath, but he managed a tiny smile. "I was, wasn't I?"

The police had taken the thieves away to the station, and Hi and the girls clustered around the television star, thanking him for his timely help.

"I especially liked it when you announced that your hands were registered weapons," Rocky declared, making a vicious chop into the air.

Nick chuckled. "That was a good one." He winked at her and said, "I stole it from episode twelve of my old show."

Rocky's jaw dropped open. "You mean, your hands *aren't* registered weapons?"

"Good heavens, no!" Nick answered. "I've never taken a karate lesson in my life."

"But you had all the right moves," Rocky protested. "I would have sworn you were a black belt." She was a first-year karate student on the air force base and had seen the experts in action.

"The fight choreographer on the show taught me the basic positions," Nick explained. "The rest I picked up from watching the stuntmen. You *do* learn a thing or two when you play a role for three years."

"You sure had those guys scared," McGee added. "Especially when you told them that Sergeant Milligan was just outside the door waiting for your signal."

"Acting, my dear, pure acting." Nicholas took a sip of his lemonade. "I was scared silly."

"I'm amazed that the police came in when they did," Hi Lo said. "How did you swing that?"

The actor shook his head. "I had nothing to do with that. Someone else must have called them."

Mary Bubnik raised her hand. "I did."

"But how?" Rocky asked. "You never left the restaurant."

"Ah." Hi raised one finger and smiled knowingly. "The little red button behind the counter. I forgot that you knew about it, Mary Bubnik."

"So did I," Mary Bubnik giggled. "But in all the commotion my knee accidentally hit it."

"And it sent a direct signal to the police station," Hi explained.

"Well, I, for one, believed that Sergeant Milligan had the building surrounded and was out there waiting for your signal to come in and arrest the bad guys," Rocky said with admiration.

"Me, too," Gwen declared. "I believed every word you said."

"Why, thank you!" Nick bowed his head in her direction. "That's the highest praise you can give an actor." Then he muttered darkly, "I only hope the critics will be as generous when they see our show."

"Correction," Gwen said, raising a finger. "*Your* show. We were fired, remember?"

"Oh, dear, that's right. After that unfortunate business with the scenery." Nick clucked sympathetically. "I myself am glad it happened. The painting of the palace on that wall was just awful, and so old-fashioned, too. I really should thank you girls for that — and for saving my life, which is why I followed you here in the first place. That was a near thing with that pillar, you know."

"Don't thank us," Rocky said. "Thank McGee. She's the one who fell off the platform."

"But Rocky's the one who told you to look out," Mary Bubnik pointed out. "And kept you from being wiped out by that column."

To Rocky's surprise Nicholas Blade reached out and, grasping her hand, bowed over it elegantly.

129

"You have my heartfelt gratitude. Is there anything I could do for you in return?"

"Well, there *is* something . . ." Rocky shook her head. "Naw, it's too late."

"What?" Nick prodded. "Go on, tell me."

"Well . . ." Rocky grinned shyly. "It would be nice if you could get us back in the show."

"And have that mean old director yell at us some more?" Mary Bubnik gasped. "Why?"

Rocky frowned. "Because of the Bunheads."

"The Bunheads!" Gwen repeated. "I forgot all about them."

"You see, if we're not in the show," Rocky explained, "they'll find out that we were fired, and they'll never let us live it down."

"Now, back up a minute," Nick interrupted, raising his hand. "Who are these Bunheads?"

"Oooh, they're these awful snobs in our ballet class at the academy," Zan explained.

"They think they're better than us," Rocky fumed, "just because they got cast in the *Sleeping Beauty* ballet."

"They *are* better than us," McGee moaned. "You don't see *them* getting fired."

Rocky banged her fist on the counter. "I'd like to do the play, just to show them!"

Mary Bubnik turned to Nick and added, "Besides, Mr. Blade, you should hear what they said about you."

"I can just imagine," Nick murmured.

"They said you couldn't remember your lines, and that the play was going to be a disaster, and that —"

"Mary!" Zan shot Mary Bubnik a warning look. "Mr. Blade doesn't need to hear *all* of what they said."

"Well, they're partly right," Nick confessed. "I have been having trouble with my lines lately. It's silly, too, because I really do know them." Nick rubbed his eyes in frustration. "If I can just get the first words of each scene, then I'm home free. But for some reason, I go blank."

"What about a prompter offstage?" Rocky suggested.

"Yeah, they could whisper the line to you from the wings," McGee added.

"I've thought of that, but there's a slight drawback." He tapped his ears lightly. "My hearing's not what it used to be. The prompter would be too far away to do me any good." Nick shook his head sadly. "No, I'd almost need someone right there beside me."

"That *is* a problem," Hi said, rubbing his chin thoughtfully. "They'd have to be invisible."

"Or part of the play, somehow," McGee added.

Nick sighed and said, "Well, I'll just have to try harder and hope the play isn't a disaster, as your friends the Bunheads put it." He turned to Hi and rubbed his hands together. "In the meantime, Mr.

Lo, you wouldn't have anything back in that kitchen of yours that we might eat, would you? I'm positively famished."

"I did have my Hi Lo Ice Cream Soufflé but" — Hi pointed sadly at the mess littering the floor of the restaurant — "unfortunately, it's deflated."

"That soufflé helped those crooks," Gwen observed. "It was great the way the ice cream shot out and blinded that ugly guy."

"Yes, well . . ." Hi rubbed his hands on his apron and grinned sheepishly. "It wasn't supposed to explode like that. But I'm not sure what I'm doing wrong."

"If you don't mind a suggestion from me," Nick offered, "perhaps I can help solve your problem. Delving into the culinary arts is my little specialty." Nick had already grabbed an apron off a hook and looped it over his head.

"Culinary arts?" Mary whispered to Zan. "What does that mean?"

"Cooking."

"Nicholas Blade, P.I., is a cook?" Rocky blurted out in disbelief.

"Chef is the proper word," he corrected her. "But whatever name you call it — cooking is a great art."

"Mr. Blade, please," Hi protested, "I wouldn't dream of asking a guest to cook."

"Nonsense, old fellow," Nick interrupted. "I'll have you know that once, when I was between acting jobs,

132

I worked as *chef de pâtisserie* for Jean-Louis Chevreau."

Hi looked stunned. "Not *the* Jean-Louis Chevreau? The greatest chef in America?"

Nick smiled proudly. "None other. And I am proud to say that my pastries are legendary among theatrical circles."

Hi bowed deeply at the waist. "My kitchen is honored by your presence."

Nick bowed just as low. "The honor is mine, sir." He clapped his hands and looked at Hi expectantly. "Now, shall we get to it? I need flour, eggs, confectioner's sugar, lots of butter, and one or two other little things."

The girls watched in amazement as Nick swept through the kitchen like a whirlwind. Before they knew it he had baked a tray full of delicate little triangles of dough filled with strawberry jam.

"Et voilà!" Nick announced as he set the tray in front of them. "The perfect late-night snack."

Gwen was the first to try the pastries. As she bit into the buttery crust, she crossed her eyes with pleasure. "Wow! These are heavenly, Mr. Blade."

The others dove in greedily and pronounced their own tart to be the best they'd ever tasted.

"I still can't believe that Nicholas Blade is a cook," Rocky said as she licked the crumbs off her fingers. "But I'm sure glad you are."

"Let me tell you a secret," Nick told her. "I like to

cook a hundred times more than I like to act." He grimaced and added, "Especially these days, when it's getting harder and harder to remember my lines. I *never* forget a recipe." He smiled slyly. "Nor do I forget to repay a good turn." He folded his arms and declared, "Girls, I'm going to see to it that you're back in the show."

"You are?" Zan cried.

"Really?" Gwen echoed.

Nick nodded.

"But how are you going to get the director to unfire us?" Mary Bubnik asked.

"I'll tell him that I won't go on unless you five are there with me." Nick stuck out his chest and held on to the lapels of his leather jacket. "I *am* the star of the show." Then he arched an eyebrow in Mary's direction. "Even though I have gotten old and bald and fat, as you once put it."

The gang stared at the floor in embarrassment. "We didn't mean it, Mr. Blade," Mary Bubnik apologized. "It's just that you looked different than you do on TV, that's all. We weren't used to you."

"Well, now that you're used to me, what do you think?"

"You're the greatest!" Rocky gave the actor a high five. She still couldn't get over how terrific he had looked when he battled the hoods. Especially since he had never taken a day of karate in his life.

"Why, thank you," he said with a chuckle.

"No, thank *you* for getting us back in the show," Gwen corrected.

"Don't thank me, yet," Nick cautioned them. "We'll see how my lines go on opening night."

"I've been thinking about your memory problem," Zan said in her soft voice. "And I think I've come up with a solution." She held up her lavender pad which she had covered with notes. "This way, you'll remember your lines, and we'll be right there to help."

"Tell me, dear girl," Nick said as the gang huddled in close around her. "I'm all ears."

Chapter Thirteen

"Mr. Blade!" Rocky called as she knocked lightly on the actor's dressing room door. "It's us."

"Entrez!" a deep voice sang out from inside.

Rocky opened the door and the girls stepped inside.

"Wow!" McGee said, looking around the large, comfortable room. "This sure beats that closet they dumped us in."

Plush Persian carpets covered the floor, and a comfortable armchair sat in the corner. A small refrigerator hummed in the other corner. Nicholas Blade sat at his dressing table in full costume, carefully applying the finishing touches to his makeup in the mirror on his elegant dressing table. The corners of the table were covered with flowers and cards from well-wishers.

"Well," Nick declared, standing and facing them with his fists on his hips, "how do I look?"

His gold pants had been altered to fit him perfectly and, instead of a red sash, he now wore a wide black belt with a dazzling gold buckle around his waist. His face and arms gleamed with makeup that made him look bronzed and rugged. An elaborate medallion hung from his neck on a thick golden chain.

"Magnificent!" Zan clapped her hands together. "Just like Yul Brynner."

"But better," Mary Bubnik added.

Gwen nodded. "You look ten years younger."

Nick patted her on the shoulder. "That's just what I needed to hear. It calms my nerves."

"*You* get nervous?" Rocky asked in surprise.

"Everyone gets nervous before a show, my dear," Nick replied, slipping his arms into an ornately embroidered gold-and-black brocade jacket. "And if they say they don't, they're lying." The actor faced the full-length mirror and adjusted his jacket. "I'm glad you're here," he said. "I've been going over the first scene in the play. And the words keep going out of my head."

"First scene." Zan pointed to McGee. "That's you."

McGee checked a note card she'd slipped in her pocket and then snapped to attention. "You are schoolteacher," she whispered without moving her lips.

"Ah, yes." Nick snapped his fingers. "You are schoolteacher?" he acted in a clipped Asian accent. "You are part of general plan I have." Then he dropped his pose and said, "Et cetera, et cetera. Perfect."

Gwen peeked at her own cue card for the next scene. "Are you sure this is going to work?"

"Of course it will work," Nick replied, attaching a gold hoop to his ear that made him look like a pirate. "Just as long as one of you is there to give me my first word, everything will go smoothly."

"But won't the audience think it's a little strange that the King's children are always with him?" Mary Bubnik asked.

"They won't even notice," Nick answered. "Besides, I'm surrounded by palace guards all of the time, anyway. They'll just think you're part of the scenery."

"We agreed that once Mr. Blade gets his line, we can leave the scene," Zan reminded them.

"Right." Rocky shook her head and chuckled. "I still can't believe the director is letting us do this."

"Believe it, my dears," Nick said as he did several knee bends. "We all want the same thing — a good show." He kicked his leg up high in front of him. "If having you in all of my scenes with me is what it takes to get that, then Hayden Wilson is all for it."

He cleared his throat noisily and hummed a scale to himself. "I'll have to ask you to leave now," he said, ushering them to the door. Nick tapped his

138

throat and explained, "It's time to warm up these old pipes of mine."

"Sure thing," McGee said. "We need to go over our plan again, anyway."

"Thanks, my friends." The actor squeezed Zan's shoulder gently and smiled at the gang. "Thanks for everything."

The girls gave Nick the television detective's trademark thumbs-up in reply.

Nick laughed and called, "See you on the ice!"

"Ice?" Mary Bubnik asked once they were alone in the corridor. "What does that mean?"

"It's theatre lingo," Rocky explained. "Acting's a little like ice-skating. You never know when you're going to slip up and fall."

"Which, in Nick's case, means forgetting your lines," McGee said.

"So he's saying not to worry if things get a little scary onstage tonight," Rocky finished.

"A *little?*" Gwen repeated. "We're about to go out in front of hundreds of people in a play that we've hardly rehearsed. If you ask me, that's *really* scary."

They found the green room jammed with actors in various stages of dress and undress. Over by the coffeepot Monty was frantically trying to hot-glue a peacock feather to the headdress of one of the palace guards. Cheryl was flitting from costume to costume, snipping a stray thread here, sewing a snap on there. Dancers were doing their warm-ups in between singers humming vocal exercises.

McGee did a quick scan of the room, looking for Brett Allen. They hadn't spoken for two days and it had been agony.

"What were you girls doing in dressing room number one?" Ashley demanded. She and Dawn were checking each other's costumes in the full-length mirror by the door. "That's Mr. Blade's."

"We were just going over some last-minute acting details with Nick." Rocky polished her nails on her jacket. "He asked us to join him."

"He asked *you?*" Ashley crossed her arms and stared at them dubiously. "I don't believe it."

"Believe it," Dawn said, tugging at her friend's arm. "Didn't you see the notice on the bulletin board?"

Ashley shook her head. "What did it say?"

"It said that they were going to be in all of Mr. Blade's scenes, and that we should leave them alone backstage because they had to concentrate."

"Right." McGee put her hand to her head, pretending to think. "We've got a job to do." The rest of the girls did likewise, and Ashley and Dawn moved to the other side of the room.

"What I think is so great," Gwen whispered, once they were alone, "is that we don't have to dance in that 'Getting to Know You' number anymore."

"Or sing," Mary Bubnik added. She heaved a small sigh. "Once again, a musical director has asked me to keep my mouth shut."

"Five minutes to places, ladies and gentlemen,"

Mel's voice boomed over the backstage intercom. "Five minutes."

"Come on!" Zan leaped up and gestured for the group to follow her. "We'd better take our positions backstage and go over the strategy one more time."

"Do we have to?" Rocky groaned. "We've gone over it so many times, my brain aches."

The five of them had gotten permission from their principals to skip school that Friday. The entire day had been spent in rehearsal with the King, Anna, and the director, who'd forgiven them for the disaster with the sets.

"I think I've got the entire musical of *The King and I* memorized," Gwen said. "Including the songs."

Rocky pulled open the stage door and the gang tiptoed inside. Large set pieces were standing along the outer wall, ready to be moved on stage during the appropriate scene change. They had to duck under several large papier-mâché trees to get to the big curtain. The heavy velvet drapes had been pulled shut across the stage, but the girls could hear the orchestra tuning up in the pit and the hum of the audience as they took their seats in the auditorium.

"Let's see if we can see anybody we know." Before anyone could stop her Rocky had scurried out onto the darkened stage to the center of the curtain.

"Rocky!" Mary Bubnik hissed. "Someone might see you."

"Aw, don't be such a worrywart." Rocky felt for

the break in the curtain and opened it just wide enough to peek out. "Hey, there's my family."

Her father was leading her mother and four brothers down the center aisle to the front row. Although he was wearing civilian clothes, it was easy to pick out Sergeant Garcia as a military man by his erect bearing. Behind him Rocky could hear her brother Michael declare loudly to a woman sitting nearby that his sister was starring in the show. Her other brothers were doing the same thing.

Rocky felt a warm glow as she realized her brothers were actually proud of her.

"Let me look," Gwen said, pushing her way up to the curtain. "My mom and goony brother are supposed to be out there somewhere." She spotted her mother's blonde hair in the third row. Her brother's glasses glinted with the reflection of the overhead lights in the seat beside Mrs. Hays. "I don't believe it," Gwen gasped.

"What?" Zan asked, coming up beside her.

"My brother is eating M&M's."

"That's terrible," Mary Bubnik clucked disapprovingly. "Food's not allowed in the auditorium. It says so right above the lobby doors."

"You better believe it's terrible," Gwen growled. "Those were mine! I hid that bag in the car especially for after the show."

McGee pushed Gwen aside and said, "Let me have a turn." She scanned the auditorium for a moment. Suddenly McGee hissed, "There she is!"

"Your mom?" Mary Bubnik asked.

"No," McGee replied. "Courtney Clay! In the fifth row."

Zan stood on tiptoe, trying to peer over McGee's shoulder. "How do you know it's Courtney?"

"I'd know that bun anywhere."

"C'mon, let me see." Rocky nudged McGee to one side and peeked through the hole again. "Page and Alice are with her, too. And they've all got their hair up in those stupid buns. Make me gag!"

"I wonder if they ever let their hair down," Mary Bubnik mused. "I mean, they may have worn it like that for so long that it's permanently stuck in a bun."

"I doubt that," Zan giggled. "But it would be pretty funny if they couldn't straighten their hair out."

"Better get to places, you guys," a voice called from the side of the stage. Emmet the assistant stage manager was standing beside a control panel, wearing a headset. Behind him the girls could hear Mel's voice on the intercom in the corridor, "Ladies and gentlemen, we have places. Places for act one."

A burst of applause erupted from the audience, and the gang sprang back from the curtain.

"What was that for?" Mary Bubnik asked as they hurried offstage into the wings. "The play hasn't even started."

"That's for the conductor," Rocky explained. "He just took his place in front of the orchestra for the overture."

The wings were now full of actors and dancers

143

preparing for their first entrances. Suddenly music filled the auditorium. At the same time the lights backstage dimmed.

"This is it!" McGee whispered excitedly as the heavy red velvet curtain parted. "Our acting debut."

Rocky nodded. "With that renowned TV star —"

"And our good friend," Mary Bubnik chimed in.

The gang turned and beamed at the famous actor, who'd stepped into the wings beside them. With his head held high, he stood poised, ready to make a regal entrance.

"Nicholas Blade," Zan said proudly, "the King of Siam!"

Chapter Fourteen

"Listen to this," Hi Lo announced as the gang gathered at his restaurant for a celebration the following night. He snapped the newspaper in his hands crisply and read, "Last night's performance of *The King and I* was a shining jewel in the Deerfield theatrical season."

"All right!" Rocky raised her cup of cranberry punch that Hi had made them and led the cheering.

"Wait!" Hi gestured for them to be still. "There's more. Deborah Gregg, as Anna, led a cast that was practically perfect in every way. They sang and danced beautifully. But the uncontested star of the show was —"

"Nicholas Blade!" the girls shouted along with Hi. Nicholas, who was seated at the counter with the girls, took a sip of his punch and beamed happily. "Well, isn't that marvelous."

Hi continued reading the review. "Nicholas Blade was triumphant as the majestic, funny, sad, and always believable King."

"Not just wow," Rocky murmured. "But *wowie!*"

"Ahem!" Hi rustled the paper again for silence. "Three cheers go to the director, Hayden Wilson, who chose to have the King's children appear in so many scenes. It showed how much the ruler cared for his children and added a soft, vulnerable side to a powerful King."

"It wasn't the director's idea to put us in those scenes," Gwen huffed, slamming her cup of punch on the counter.

Nick chuckled and patted her on the back. "That's the theatre, my dear. If the play is good, the director gets all of the credit. But if it's a bomb, the actors get the blame."

"But that's not fair," Mary Bubnik protested.

"That's show biz," Nicholas replied with shrug. He turned to Hi and grinned. "This is as good a time as any to tell them my news, don't you think?"

"Absolutely," Hi agreed.

"What news?" McGee asked as she and the others leaned on the counter, all ears.

"I'm leaving the theatre," Nicholas announced solemnly.

"What?" they all cried in shock.

"You can't!" Mary Bubnik pleaded.

146

"Not after your triumph," Gwen added, using the critic's own words from the review.

"The best time to leave is after a triumph," Nicholas Blade said, rising to his feet. "Then people will always say I quit at the peak of my career."

Mary Bubnik slumped with her elbows on the counter. "I can't believe that there'll be no more Nicholas Blade, P.I."

"Ah, but there will be," Nicholas declared with a twinkle in his eye. He strode over to the back door of the restaurant, where a large board stood, covered with a white tablecloth.

Hi joined him and they each grabbed one corner of the material. "Whenever you're ready," Hi said to the actor.

Nicholas gave the signal and they whipped the tablecloth into the air. *"Et voilà!"*

Leaning against the wall was a wooden sign, with a painting of a jolly chef in a white apron and tall hat, holding a steaming tray of brightly colored tarts fresh out of the oven. The steam curled up into the air, spelling out in ornate lettering:

Nicholas Blade, Pastries Incorporated

"You're opening a restaurant?" Zan exclaimed.

Nicholas nodded vigorously. "I've been discussing it with my good friend Hi, here, for the past two days.

He's the one who suggested the idea. After all, I love to bake — so why not do it for a living?"

"I think it's a great idea," Gwen said, remembering the little pastries he had cooked for them the other evening. "I'll be your first customer."

"Right you are, Gwendolyn." Nick slipped a white chef's hat on his head and saluted jauntily. "I've got the Nicholas Blade Special in the kitchen right now, all prepared and ready to eat." He rubbed his hands together eagerly. "Wait right here."

"The Nicholas Blade Special?" Rocky whispered. "That wouldn't be like the latest Hi Lo Specials, would it?"

Hi pushed his glasses to the end of his nose and asked indignantly, "And what do you mean by that?"

Gwen finished the remains of her cranberry punch and wiped the red moustache off her lip. "She means, can it be used as a lethal weapon?"

"Yeah," McGee added, trying to keep a straight face. "Can you throw it like a discus?"

Zan giggled softly. "Or does it explode like a grenade?"

"To all those questions, no," Nicholas called as he swung open the kitchen door. In his hand he carried a large frying pan with cherries bubbling in a jelly sauce. Nicholas picked up a bottle of brandy, poured some into the pan, and swirled it around. Then Nick struck a kitchen match and declared, "This one ignites!"

He touched the burning match to the contents of the pan, and suddenly the entire dessert burst into blue flames.

Zan and Mary Bubnik screamed. McGee fell backward off her stool. Rocky fumbled for her glass of water to put it out while Gwen covered her head and screeched, "Call 911!"

Hi and Nicholas burst out laughing at the girls' reaction. Tears streamed down Hi's cheeks. He took off his glasses and rubbed his eyes, saying, "That's called Flaming Cherries Jubilee. You're *supposed* to light it."

"Well," McGee said, getting up off the floor and dusting off her jeans, "you should warn people that you're going to torch your food. Some people might have gotten scared."

The girls watched in amazement as Nicholas poured the liquid fire over individual servings of vanilla ice cream.

"Why go to all that trouble to make this," Gwen asked as the fire slowly flickered out, "if you're just going to burn it up?"

"It's not burnt," Nicholas replied, handing a spoon to Gwen. "It's just hot. Taste it."

Gwen dug the spoon into the cherry-and-ice-cream mixture and popped it in her mouth. The others watched her carefully as she closed her eyes and groaned, "Heaven!"

The bell over the door tinkled, and a familiar voice

called, "Is this a private party, or can anybody join?"

"Brett!" Nicholas waved his hand. "Come on in."

The boy gestured toward the street. "I've got most of the cast with me. Is that okay?"

"The more the merrier," Hi cried as he scurried behind the counter.

In a trice the tiny restaurant was packed with people, all talking at once. Several actors held up copies of the newspaper and read the rave review over and over to their friends. A line instantly formed by the punch bowl and at the counter. Hi bustled about preparing drinks for his guests while Nicholas hurried back into the kitchen to prepare more rounds of Cherries Jubilee.

When McGee heard Nicholas call Brett's name her first impulse had been to run. If she could get out the door, she wouldn't have to face him. She forced herself to turn around. When she did, she found herself staring directly into Brett's piercing blue eyes.

"You're terrific in the play," McGee said finally. Then she gulped and added, "And that's no lie."

"Thanks." Brett shoved his hands in his pockets and kicked at the floor. "Listen," he said. "About calling you a liar . . ."

McGee held up one hand. "It was my own fault." She paused, realizing that now she'd have to explain why she lied to him. McGee squeezed her eyes shut and let the words pour out. "Listen, I don't usually lie, in fact, usually I'm very truthful. But I told you I didn't like sports because, well, I didn't want you to think I was just a baseball player."

McGee held her breath, waiting for him to respond. Finally she opened her eyes and Brett asked, "What's wrong with baseball?"

"Nothing," McGee said with a shrug. "It's just that, um . . ." She stared at her hands. "Some guys think girls who play sports are tomboys."

"Not me," Brett replied with a smile. "I'm just the opposite. I like girls who are athletic and straightforward."

McGee looked up at him in surprise. "Yeah?"

"Yeah." Brett pointed toward the back booth, where Hi had placed the punch bowl. "Let's get something to drink."

"Sure." McGee walked beside him toward the refreshments. They passed Ashley and Dawn, who sang out coyly, "We watched you from the wings last night. Did you see us?"

"No, sorry, I didn't," Brett said politely as he and McGee stepped up to the punch bowl.

"You looked soooooo cute," Dawn said. Then she covered her mouth and erupted into high-pitched giggling.

Brett's face turn pink, and he turned away stiffly to the punch bowl. As he poured McGee a glass of juice, he whispered. "It's girls who act so squirrelly that I can't stand."

"Me, too," McGee whispered, taking a sip of her drink. "Say, did you hear about the Reds game last night?"

"You bet." Brett downed his punch in one gulp. "I had my dad tape it on our VCR."

"Man, I wish I could have seen it," McGee exclaimed, hopping on one of the red leather stools at the counter. "I hear Grotowski was in top form."

"Look, if you're not doing anything tomorrow," Brett suggested as he leaned against the counter, "why don't you come over to my house and watch it?"

McGee flashed a grin that spread from ear to ear. "I'd love to." She didn't know how things would turn out with Brett, but she didn't care. For now, he was her friend and she felt great just being herself again.

"I don't believe it," Gwen suddenly hissed from the far end of the counter. "Look who's at the door."

Rocky spun on her stool. She watched as Courtney, Page, and Alice wove their way through the crowd. "The Bunheads," Rocky snarled. "Trying to crash *our* party." She pushed up the sleeves of her jacket. "I'm going to tell them they're not invited."

"Wait," Zan whispered out of the corner of her mouth. "See what they want first."

Courtney, her eyes darting nervously from side to side, stepped up to the counter. "May I speak to you a moment?" she asked without looking at them.

The gang looked at each other then back at the Bunheads. "Fire away," Rocky replied.

Courtney glanced over her shoulder to make sure no one was looking and then quickly thrust a piece of paper across the counter to Rocky. "Would you ask Mr. Blade for his autograph?"

"Why don't you do it yourself?" Gwen replied. She gestured with her thumb toward the kitchen. "He's right over there."

Courtney's eyes widened in horror. "I couldn't. I don't know him."

A sly smile crossed Rocky's lips. "Why don't you have your mother ask him? Since she has so much influence."

Courtney stared hard at the floor, her nostrils flaring in and out. "My mother's the one who forced me to come in here. This autograph is for her."

Zan decided that they had let Courtney squirm long enough. "Don't worry," she said, "we'll get it for you."

"Yeah, Nick's our personal friend," Mary Bubnik said proudly. She looked at Page and Alice and asked, "Would y'all like to meet him?"

"Meet him?" Page's eyes lit up. "All of us?"

"Sure," Rocky said grandly. "Even your mother, Courtney."

Courtney's face burst into a big smile that just as quickly faded. "This wouldn't be one of your pranks, would it?"

"Of course not," Gwen replied. "Go get her, and we'll introduce you."

"Oh, thank you, guys!" Courtney clasped her

hands in front of her. "You don't know how much this means to me." She started to run for the door, then stopped and turned back. "And if there's anything I can do for you —"

"Anything?" Rocky raised an eyebrow.

"Anything," Courtney repeated. She put her hand over her heart and added, "I promise. Just ask."

As Courtney ran back through the crowd, Rocky ordered, "Zan, get out your pad and pen."

"What for?" McGee asked while Zan rifled through her tapestry bag.

Rocky rubbed her hands together. "We need to make a list of all the things we want Courtney to do for us."

Gwen shoved her glasses up on her nose and leaned into their huddle. "Great idea."

"Let's see." Rocky chewed on her nail for a second and then pointed at the pad. "Start by having her polish our ballet shoes."

Mary Bubnik shook her head. "Boy, Courtney's going to regret this."

The five friends grinned wickedly at each other and chorused, "For as long as she lives!"

Bad News Ballet

Coming soon:

#8 Camp Clodhopper

Zan slumped down on the nearest rock and watched as Courtney and the rest of the Bunheads canoed toward their shore.

"How dare you follow us up here!" Gwen called from the edge of the pier.

"Follow you?" Courtney repeated. "That's a laugh." She tilted her chin. "For your information, I go to Camp *Scotsdale*. And personally, I can't believe Camp Clodhopper is still in existence."

Rocky narrowed her eyes at Courtney. "Clod-hopper?"

"Of course. Some stupid guy named Claude Harper started it ages ago," Courtney explained in a smug tone, "but it's always been known as Camp Clodhopper to everyone."

"Why is that?" Mary Bubnik asked.

"Because it's full of clods who can't sing or dance," Courtney replied, as Page and Alice snickered loudly from their canoe.